FICTION

LESTER JANE.

THE HOUSE AT CHELTONWOOD

SPECIAL MESSAGE TO READERS

This book is published by

THE ULVERSCROFT FOUNDATION

a registered charity in the U.K., No. 264873

The Foundation was established in 1974 to provide funds to help towards research, diagnosis and treatment of eye diseases. Below are a few examples of contributions made by THE ULVERSCROFT FOUNDATION:

A new Children's Assessment Unit at Moorfield's Hospital, London.

•

Twin operating theatres at the Western Ophthalmic Hospital, London.

•

The Frederick Thorpe Ulverscroft Chair of Ophthalmology at the University of Leicester.

•

Eye Laser equipment to various eye hospitals.

If you would like to help further the work of the Foundation by making a donation or leaving a legacy, every contribution, no matter how small, is received with gratitude. Please write for details to:

THE ULVERSCROFT FOUNDATION,
**The Green, Bradgate Road, Anstey,
Leicester LE7 7FU. England
Telephone: (0533) 364325**

THE HOUSE
AT CHELTONWOOD

The loveliness of the spot and the house took Max Jefferson's breath away, and yet he had to tell the Buckland family that it was all to be swept away. For all his wealth, Max felt poor compared to the happy talented Bucklands, and longed to enter their family, especially when he fell in love with one of the girls. But Max was the enemy, and it would be a fight to convince them.

JANE LESTER

THE HOUSE AT CHELTONWOOD

Complete and Unabridged

LINFORD
Leicester

First published in Great Britain in 1983 by
Robert Hale Limited
London

First Linford Edition
published September 1991

British Library CIP Data

Lester, Jane *1913 –*
    The house at Cheltonwood. — Large print ed. —
Linford romance library
I. Title
823.914

ISBN 0–7089–7100–8

Published by
F. A. Thorpe (Publishing) Ltd.
Anstey, Leicestershire
Set by Words & Graphics Ltd.
Anstey, Leicestershire
Printed and bound in Great Britain by
T. J. Press (Padstow) Ltd., Padstow, Cornwall

1

MAXSTEAD JEFFERSON drove slowly down the hill, towards Bricketts Green, wishing he could go at this moment anywhere else. The summer evening was heavy with scents of the hedgerow and when he pulled into the side to let a small tractor squeeze by, going home, he briefly envied the driver, who looked as if he hadn't a care in the world. Probably hadn't, Maxstead thought sourly, though he hadn't wealth and was looking enviously down at the expensive car that was pulling in to let him pass. Maxstead thought the man was welcome to the car, his fine tailoring, his height, breadth and good looks, everything, if only to be able to get out and walk in this soft beautiful countryside at this moment and feel that he need not pursue this journey. And then he remembered whom this stretch of fine countryside belonged to and he scowled and stopped wishing he could walk along its quiet narrow roads. It all belonged to Isolde.

He was conscious, too, of Tim's sidelong glance at him every so often. Tim Roberts was more a friend than his estate agent and both young men were of an age — twenty-eight — the only difference being that Tim was thin and good-looking and, like the country-man who had been blissfully driving the tractor towards home, he wasn't rich, but, unlike the countryman, he had got a lot of cares. Cares Tim shouldn't have. They weren't really his. He was just helping his friend to shoulder them.

And now Tim watched his old friend switch the blinker to the left and murmured, "The right turn, for the house at Cheltonwood, Max."

"As if I didn't know. I was hoping you wouldn't notice, till it was too far to turn back."

Tim sighed. "Max, I'd do this visit

for you if I could. If I *dared*. But you know Isolde said *you* were to, and you know what she's like lately."

"But what's she want to turn them out for? They pay up their ground-rent, don't they? I know I've been abroad for ages, but have I lost touch that much?"

Tim sought uneasily for the right words. "I think she's had a bigger offer for the land than she'll admit, and this is the only house on it, and . . . well, I suppose she feels that they shouldn't stop her making a sale. She said she'd find them another house."

"Do you believe that?" Max gritted.

"Well, if she doesn't, I will. Only . . . when you see the place, I think you'll agree with me that it won't quite be the same for them, to be pushed into another house. Look out, sharp turn right. There! That's the place."

Max pulled the car into the side and stared. It wasn't an ordinary house by any means. "Why, it's a . . . a *mill*, isn't it?"

Now they could hear the water and the noise of the mill-wheel and, above it, a piano being played. "Part of it's a mill. One of the Bucklands (I think the one that died last year) built the house around it. Unusual, isn't it?"

"It's . . . beautiful," Max muttered. "And she wants this to be torn down, and these people to be turned out . . . oh, no, Tim, we must have come to the wrong place."

He got out and stood looking. Now he could smell the haunting sweetness of tobacco-plant and night-scented stock, late roses, the hundred and one old fashioned flowers a good gardener can find to make the place a riot of colour and smell, right through the summer. Trees (now in the dusk he could hardly recognise one from the other) massed around and behind the house. On impulse he put on his headlamps, to see the place better, then wished he hadn't, for the front door opened and figures erupted. First, a small one, holding on to a great hound, which was showing it didn't care for visitors at this hour, who flooded the house with headlamps from a car.

"That's a little girl holding that dog," Tim murmured. "Put your lights out, Max, or it'll pull her into the mill-stream. It's young Amy."

Max put his headlamps out and walked forward. "Take your dog in. I'm come from Lady Powley, to see your father, or whoever's in charge."

A thin boy of about fourteen stood just behind Amy, protectively, Max felt. Brown as a berry, lean and fit, a sensitive type. "I'm Stephen Buckland. Will I do? Our uncle's ill at the moment."

"No, of course you won't, silly," the third figure said. She wasn't much taller than the boy, petite and lovely, but not quite so dark. Her reddish-brown hair cascaded over her shoulders and her lovely face was half turned towards the house, so that the light from the hall fell on it. "Let's leave it to Carly. Here she comes."

"Look here," Max said. "I shouldn't have come at this hour, but I've been all round the estate and was going home, and thought I'd do this visit as I was passing. Are you sure I can't see your uncle?"

Carly didn't erupt from the house as the others had done, yet oddly Max felt she might just as well have. She wasn't good-looking like the other three but the force of her personality was tremendous. It was she who made the dog quiet, turned them all inside and said at the same time, "I quite understand, Mr Roberts, that you have your job to do, as and when you can. It can't be much fun being estate agent to our ground landlord. It *is* Mr Roberts, isn't it?"

Max glanced back at the car. Tim, the coward, had stayed there, and of course the girl had presumed that Max himself was the agent, as he had been driving the car. He didn't answer directly, but said, "I'm sorry this business call has to be made, and so late, but the owner . . . "

"Oh, come inside, do," Carly said. "I'll attend to it. Uncle Fergus is really too unwell to be bothered." She nodded to the others to go back to the kitchen. Warmth and light came out from there, but she took Max into a room that was obviously a parlour, kept as a best room, the only used thing in it being a piano, with music scattered around. "I think Jay must have finished her practice," she said, half to herself, as she put the light on and indicated a stiff armchair for him. "Now, Mr Roberts. I'm Carlotta Buckland, and I can deal with whatever it is."

He was quite sure she could and, now he saw her in the full light, the carefully prepared speech fled and he waited for her to sit down.

She couldn't have been more than twenty, yet she had the air of a person in charge. She wasn't well-groomed, but her casual clothes and hair style suited her. He couldn't remember afterwards just what she had been wearing, except that it was simple, much washed and covered by an apron she'd forgotten she was still wearing. It was her calm capable manner, her serene yet firm young face under its riot of dark curling short hair, and the brilliant blue of her eyes under long dark lashes and straight dark brows, that captivated him. A comfortable, capable girl, with the right sort of back for burdens, just the right sort of shoulder to cry on. Now what on earth had made him think that, he wondered?

"I think perhaps you'd better answer a few questions, if you don't mind, before I tell you what I've come for."

"The ground-rent's paid," she began, "and we have permission — " but he waved her to listen. "I wanted to know how many rooms there are in this rather unusual home."

"Oh?" The uptilted question suggested he should know, as the agent, just how many rooms there were. Guarded now, she said shortly, "Nine."

"Nine," he repeated. "But it looks like a mill."

"You must be new at your job," she said, managing to make the statement just that, without sounding ill mannered. "I meant the ground-rent was paid. My father bought the mill, leasehold, and added to it. He added a room with each child."

She got up. "You'd better let me show you over the place. I can only think someone has said it looks ramshackle. I want you to be sure it isn't — it just looks a bit like that from outside. I can show you everywhere except Uncle Fergus's bedroom, because he isn't well. Oh, and Holly's room — she is probably just going to sleep. She's only six."

"Holly?"

"Well, her name is really Laura Hollington Buckland, but our mother's name was Laura too, so Holly it had to be." And she led the way out, but he had the impression that her face crumpled for a brief second, before with lightning control she had composed it again. Tim had mentioned someone dying last year: presumably that would be the father, but had the mother died too? Had tragedy and bereavement struck this family so recently and was Isolde hounding them already to leave their home?

She said, "The original building, the mill, that is, still has wood walls, but . . . we plastered the new ones," and she quickly and briefly showed him the nine rooms. She hadn't included the kitchen, nor the two shower-rooms. "You should have come in daylight," she told him. "Most of our rooms look out over the back, to where the mill-stream opens out. It's a . . . beautiful view," and she showed him bedrooms that were, to his mind, both charming and, in view of the obvious shortage of spare cash, clever. Three walls in each room were encased in either cupboards, book-shelves or a combination of each, which enabled the floor to be kept tidy and provided the necessary furniture. Bunks were in three of the rooms and it wasn't difficult to see which was Stephen's — a boy's room. "Stephen has a brother?" he asked, then wished he hadn't.

She said, "My father used the other bunk, after our mother died. He couldn't bear his own room," and silently she threw open the door on the other side of the circular landing.

Max felt terrible. This room was evidently kept, with great effort, just as it always had been. The room of a woman with taste, a feminine woman. It really was a bedroom, with good pieces of furniture and pretty hangings, though obviously economy had predominated here, too. Still, the effect was quite charming. He turned away, raising a hand which indicated he was sorry he had looked in, and wanted to see no more.

"My room, and Jay's," she said briefly, a little bitterly, he thought as if to protest at the violating of the family's privacy. Although she had suggested it, she obviously had felt forced to do so.

He briefly looked at a slightly more feminine version of the boy's room. The third room with bunks was occupied obviously by the two little girls, and where the smaller girl was probably just asleep. They turned towards the stairs in silence, Carly merely indicating the other unopened door, presumably the uncle's room.

As they were about to descend, he must have heard them, and opened it. Max frowned. The tall soldierly figure with the prematurely white hair and military moustaches, and the arrogant hawk nose, was not unknown to him but he couldn't remember where he had seen it before. The older man said quietly, evidently remembering the sleeping child, "Who have you here, Carlotta, at this time of night?"

With a resigned air, Carly took Max across the landing again, saying softly, "I'm sorry, Uncle Fergus. I thought you'd be asleep. I can handle this. It's only Lady Powley's agent. He wanted to see the house. He's new to the job."

The two men very briefly acknowledged the introduction. He knows who I am, Max thought, irritably, and wondered why he didn't want Carly to know. Sheltering behind Tim's name, he told himself, in disgust. Well, it was true. He would rather be Tim than himself, any day, and he didn't want Carlotta Buckland to look at him with contempt. She would never understand that it was no wish of his to turn people out.

The uncle's white eyebrows shot up, he looked at Max quizzically, waiting, no doubt, for Carly's remark to be corrected. Max stuck to his resolution to say nothing until he was forced to.

Carly said gently, "Go back to bed, Uncle Fergus. Not to worry. Everything's under control."

"No, indeed it isn't," Fergus Buckland said. "Come into my room, both of you. By the way, who's still in the car?" He slowly went to the window, as Max didn't reply, then moved back and said obscurely, "Oh, I see. Now, sir, just what is it you want with us? You must know we own this house and pay ground-rent. And it is paid."

"Yes. Yes, I know," Max said hastily. "It's just that Lady Powley requested me to come and . . . "

"Did she, indeed!" Fergus Buckland sounded slightly contemptuous.

It was no use, Max saw. He would have to deliver the blow. If he didn't, Isolde might take it into her head to come herself, and that might be disastrous. She would bring Winters, that bright young solicitor she had got herself. What was wrong with the old firm? Too fair to people like this family? Without giving himself time to think, Max said, "Lady Powley has had an offer for the land, and this is the only house on it."

Fergus Buckland put a hand blindly behind him to find the back of a chair and, having found it, kept himself upright and took what must have been a blow for him. "You mean we are to get out?" He could be just as blunt.

Max heard Carlotta gasp and she hurried forward, but her uncle snapped, "Leave me alone, girl. I'm all right. Just something I hadn't thought about. I should have, though. Enough rumours flying about, regarding this derelict land of Lady Powley's."

Carly looked reproachfully at Max. "I told you my uncle wasn't well."

"I'm sorry, but I have my job to do," Max said, ignoring the uncle's derisive snort. "If it means anything to either of you, I intend to do my best to block this crazy idea. I think it's criminal to destroy a house like this."

"Do you now!" Fergus remarked, a glint in his eye.

"And criminal to blandly say that another house will be found for the family."

"Do go on," Fergus invited, sitting down and looking less shocked. "And why should you take such an opposite stand to Lady Powley?"

"Uncle," Carly pleaded, very much embarrassed and not understanding the way the two men glared at each other.

"Perhaps because I consider this a much more desirable place to live in than, say, Powley Court," Max said.

"But you don't live at Powley Court," Fergus remarked, now enjoying this, as Max reddened.

"And why didn't Roberts come and do the job instead of skulking in the car? Couldn't face us, no doubt?"

"But Uncle, dear, this *is* Mr Roberts," Carly protested, anxiously.

"No, it isn't," Fergus said brusquely, and looked as if he were going to say just who Max was.

"My name is Maxstead Jefferson," he said quickly, to Carly. "You made a natural mistake, as apparently you didn't know Tim. Your uncle does. And Tim didn't come and do the job himself, as you put it, Mr Buckland, because I was told to, specially."

"And you always do as you're told?" Fergus asked, those eyebrows lifting again.

"No, but this time, I was passing and

had a desire to see the place that is raising such a dust, and when I did see it . . .

"Ye — es?"

"Well, it seemed such a confounded pity. I decided to take a hand in it."

"And what do you think you can do, from your exalted place in your small flat?" Fergus asked, deliberately taunting.

"That was not necessary," Max said. "The fact that my grandfather and your father were friends," he said, remembering now where he had seen that face and heard the things that were said about the owner, "gives you no right, sir, to comment on my life and the way I live it. And if I hadn't decided to do as *I* was told and come to give you notice, Lady Powley would have come herself, heavily reinforced. I don't think you'd have cared for that, any of you."

Fergus seemed suddenly tired, or perhaps it was the reminder of that old friendship of fifty years ago. "No, perhaps you're right. But it won't make any difference. We'll have to go." He looked up, angry, and met his niece's eye. "What Lady Powley wants, she must have."

"In this case, not perhaps necessarily," Max said icily. "It may just be, this time, what I happen to want."

Fergus looked as if he were doubting that. He now looked tired and very unwell. Max again apologised for the time and unheralded state of the visit and hastily made his departure.

At the bottom of the rather attractive winding wooden staircase, Carly turned to him. "Would you like to clarify the position, Mr Jefferson? You are not the agent. He is in the car. How come my uncle knows him and I don't?"

He shrugged. "I believe Tim said he meets your uncle in Trowstock. Look, I really am sorry it happened this way. I didn't want it to. I did try to get out of coming, as a matter of fact; the job seemed such an unpleasant one. But now I'm glad I've come. I wish you hadn't heard in such a sudden way, but

I will do my best to prevent ... the evacuation. I promise you."

"How can you, and why should you?" she asked coldly, still smarting because he had let her think he was Tim Roberts, while her uncle seemed to know a lot more about the whole business than she did.

"Well, let's say I've an eye for beauty. Heaven help me, I've done a bit of sketching in my time, and I'd hate to see all this go. May I come in the daylight and see it properly?"

There had been a brief glint in her eyes when he mentioned the sketching, but she was unforgiving again. "I don't see how I can stop you, Mr Jefferson," she said coldly, and turned to the front door. "But do tell me: what will Lady Powley say when you tell her how you feel about the place, and turning us out?"

That, too, was worrying Max, but he pushed it to the back of his mind. "I'll think of something," he promised, but he was promising himself, not Carly.

2

TIM said nervously, halfway home, "Dare I ask how it went?" Max had been sunk into a heavy silence while driving.

"Tim, how come they don't know you?"

Tim looked alarmed. "They do! Who says they don't?"

"They thought I was Tim Roberts. Well, at least, the one they call Carly thought that, till her uncle got me in a corner, and was just going to see that she knew my connection with Isolde, so I nipped in and gave my name. I asked her how she came to think I was Tim Roberts, and it appears she was unaware that her uncle always sees the agent in Trowstock."

Tim looked acutely embarrassed. "Well, the fact is, I crashed in there one day and made the acquaintance of the pretty one — Jay. I knew they'd all hate me if they thought I was the dreaded agent, so I didn't tell them. They just know me by my second name — Richard. I say, don't look so furious. I know it complicates things, but it is in my private time, after all. For some reason that isn't difficult to guess, they loathe their ground landlord and everyone else they've come up against while they've tried to make a home there. So I'm just known as Richard (Jay's friend) and there's an amiable conspiracy not to let the uncle know. She's not supposed to be . . . having friends outside."

"Why not?" Max asked bluntly.

Tim looked anxious and bothered and embarrassed, all at once, as Max pulled up outside a pub and said, "Let's have a pint and talk. There's a lot I need to know before I face Isolde tonight."

"You haven't forgotten she's giving a party, I suppose?"

21

"Oh, help, yes, I had. Well, I don't have to be there."

"Yes, you do. So do I, as the dogsbody, thank heavens. I can escape."

"What makes you think I can't?" Max asked, his mind still on Carly.

"If you want to save your friends from the chop, you'd better keep on the right side of Isolde," Tim warned. "You know what she's like. Let her think you're giving her her own way, and you're home and dry."

"It's a good thing you're my best friend, saying a thing like that," Max remarked, but his eyes were flinty. He had been very difficult just lately. Tim said anxiously, "I'm on your side, Max."

"And no doubt you want me to be on yours?"

"Well, I'd hate it if you let on that I'm, well, pretty keen on Jay Buckland."

They took their drinks away from the bar and found a quiet corner. "This Jay Buckland, why such an outlandish name?"

"Her name is Jewel. Who'd want a name like that? Jay's just the initial really. She's ... a lovely girl," Tim said.

"And I understand there's a small child called Holly because her name was Laura, same as the mother's. Mother now dead, I take it?"

Tim glanced quickly at him. "I say, you don't know much of local history, do you? The mother's death was rather mysterious. Well, it was finally called an accident, but one of those accidents that always leave a doubt when the gossips get going. The father was rather upset."

"Well, I imagine he would be, in a family like that. They seem close-knit," Max said. His had not been a happy life. He tended to be interested in people who managed to look close-knit and happy.

"The father was a charming chap but a bit of a ... well, fact is, he was horse-mad. Always betting. Worried the mother sick. So she punished him by calling every new child after a horse he'd lost heavily on. Carlotta, for instance. And . . . Jewel. Amy, too — that was a horse called Amora."

"Well, what a devilish thing to do!" Max exploded.

"Oh, I don't know. At the end of her tether, poor woman. She worked frightfully hard to scrape a living — artist, you know. You must have seen those delicate mill drawings in the town. Anscombe's shop sells them. Don't do bad in the tourist season, but not much going as a regular income. Still, she tried. Must have been discouraging every time the husband took the proceeds to put on a horse and lost."

"Didn't he ever win?"

"Yes, a tidy sum, when Holly was born. That's why she didn't get a horse name. Took her mother's name and family name. Much good it did her. She died when Holly was four. He was lost without her. Roamed around doing nothing much, and caught it in a road accident, last year." Tim stared into his beer as if he couldn't imagine how it got there. "Just a year after his wife. Missed her. Not much use carrying on, he told me once."

"Oh, he knew you!"

Tim looked upset briefly. "Jay asked me to keep an eye on him. So I went into his favourite places. We got talking. We got on. He wasn't a bad chap."

"Who's Jay like? The mother? Pretty girl, I recall, from what I saw of her."

"No. Like her old man. Very handsome chap, he was. And always so surprised that people got fed up with him. I rather liked him."

Max felt an ache inside him to talk about Carlotta, but he didn't dare. Tim was no fool. So he had to work up to her by degrees. "What about the boy, Stephen?"

"Named after a horse," Tim said shortly. "Stephen of England. Almost bankrupted the lot of them. That's when the uncle came to visit them and stayed for a bit. He could see his young brother's family life wasn't going to be improved by a stranger living there. Besides, he was a writer as far back as that, and found the young family a bit hectic. He came back when his brother died, to take charge."

Max said slowly, "Did Isolde know about all this? I mean, if their income was so precarious, I wonder she didn't get the itch to throw them out ages ago."

Tim considered it. "I don't think she would have considered throwing them out until this big offer came up, to buy the land. Not much point, really. I mean, joking apart, Max, Isolde never did anything without seeing the chance to make money out of it. Talent for making money, Isolde," he added hastily.

"So who owns that house now? The uncle?"

"No," Tim said carefully. "It all went to Carlotta."

"Carlotta!"

"That's right." Tim toyed with the

handle of his mug. "The mill belonged to her mother, d'you see. Wedding present by a doting father, though he didn't leave much when he died. But it wasn't just that the mother was afraid the mill would go the way all their cash went — betting — that she left it to Carlotta. I remember she said to me once that if she had anything to leave, it would go to that elder daughter of hers, who could see a way to survive when everyone else was starving. It was Carlotta who got the mill enlarged. Persuaded a local workman to do it in his spare time, in return for stuff she grew in the garden. She's the practical gardener around here, by the way."

"Yes, but look here, she told me her father bought the mill and added a room every time a new child arrived."

Tim looked anything but happy. "Proud, Carlotta."

He looked as if he were wanting to say something else but didn't quite dare. Max said, "She isn't married," in the tone of a statement.

"Not yet," Tim said carefully. "Fact is, Foxwell, the builder chap, has got an eye on the main chance. Decided fruit and veg wasn't enough to make all this carpentry and building worth his while. So he put it to her that if he thought they were going to be man and wife, he could put some heart into it."

Max's head came up suddenly and he looked, really angry. "So she's engaged to this builder chap?

"Well, no." Tim laughed. "Carlotta's not that easy. She's the one who has to take the sketches her mother left, to Anscombe's place to sell. Know Anscombe's little shop on the corner? So Keith Anscombe got ideas too, so Carlotta is playing them off one against the other at the moment. It must be nerve-racking, especially as she dare not let the uncle know. Very stiff-necked, Fergus Buckland."

Tim wondered if he'd gone too far, Max looked so furious. Then Max suddenly got up and replenished their glasses, and came back to say, in a tight sort of voice that Tim recognised well, "So here we have the uncle, unwell, struggling to do his writing, with the burden of bringing up the family. That poor girl, Carlotta," and somehow he made the name sound rather special, in spite of his anger, "coping with selling things — herself if she's pushed hard enough — to make an income. And all those youngsters — "

"Jay is pretty hot with her needle," Tim put in hastily. "She does dress-making for a living. Well, mainly to pay for her piano lessons. She wants to go to Paris to study music."

"Well, she's got a hope, hasn't she?" Max retorted, trying to see the thing in its right perspective and not noticing Tim's quick flush. "Well, what I'm trying to work out is how Isolde could possibly — even Isolde at her worst — could possibly think of making a quick fortune out of turning that lot out, with the troubles they've got!"

"She knows, too," Tim said, staring at his beer again, in his misery. "I tried to tell her. Damned silly thing to do. Made her want it all the more. Well, I could see that, the minute I mentioned their troubles."

"Who's paying for the boy's education?" Max demanded.

"You must be joking!" He gulped, decided against apologising to the man who, besides being his friend, was also, in a way, his boss, and said, flatly, "He does his share towards scraping an income. He's got an old bike and does a paper round first thing, in Trowstock."

Max muttered something incomprehensible.

Tim said, "Amy wants to be a vet. She's crazy about animals. She can't understand how it costs so much to train. She goes in every Saturday morning to the town, to help the local man."

"And if Carlotta decided to marry the builder, would he take that lot on?" Max forced himself to ask.

Tim's look was enough.

"And we've complicated things a bit more," Max said savagely. "They don't know who I am (at least, the uncle does) and they don't know who their dear friend Richard is. Did I tell you I recognised the uncle as an old friend? Well, his father and my grandfather were buddies. I knew I'd seen that face before."

"I know, it's all a mess, Max, but we ought to go. Isolde's party."

"Ah, yes, the party," Max said, smiling a smile that Tim didn't care for at all. "Max, don't break it up, will you?" he put in anxiously, but Max said, out of his own deep-seated misery, "On the contrary, I shall go to it and be very nice to Isolde. That, I believe, is what you want? And I'll see if I can do anything for those poor devils at The Mill House."

"No, Max, I beg you," Tim pleaded. "For the sake of the people at the house at Cheltonwood, leave it alone. Leave it alone."

"Why, Maxstead Jefferson!" Nerys, Isolde's aunt stopped beside Max and Tim, who stood briefly in one of the long glass doors to the terrace at Powley Court. "It's so long since I saw my niece's husband, I swear I'd forgotten what he looked like. Handsome as usual, far too big for the little dwarfs all around him, and as bored as I remember him."

She was a well set-up woman of sixty and showed no family likeness to Isolde at all, Max thought, as he put himself out to charm her. She had never been anything but friendly to him, though she had often told him what a fool she considered him, for ever having been interested in her spoilt niece.

"Why are you here, Max? Isolde looks like the cat that's been at the cream. What's going on?"

Tim had already slid away with an apology and, as he had so much to do behind the scenes at a party such as this, nobody stopped him.

"Have you heard of the St Ann's

Project, Aunt Nerys?" he asked quietly.

"Well, what a question to ask in a place like this? And as if I'd admit to knowing anything about anything so explosive, dear boy!"

"It will make several millions for Isolde, would you think?"

She extravagantly brushed aside such a mad suggestion, but her shrewd eyes said otherwise. "Anyway, Maxstead, what do you care how much Isolde makes? She's generous to you, isn't she?"

It flicked him on the raw. He had always hated the suggestion that he was living on Isolde's fortune. "I have money of my own," he said tautly.

Aunt Nerys said, "Look, dear boy, find me a chair in that noisy corner near that atrocious dance-band, and then I'll talk, where the row they're making will drown my voice to all except you."

He doubted if she'd be very comfortable on one of the many little gilt chairs surrounding the walls for the occasion, or whether he'd hear a thing she said, above the pop-music being played. Funny, he thought, how Isolde loved to show she was 'with it', even to that extent. The great ballroom was packed and the late summer evening clammy hot, with the threat of a storm, but as with Isolde, her Aunt Nerys had to be obeyed, too, so he found her a cool drink with plenty of gin in it, the way she liked it, and sat by her.

"Now, my lad, what is your interest in this project?" Isolde's aunt demanded, so he replied with equal straightness, "It means the loss of a home to a very nice family, and sweeping away the most incredibly beautiful house built out of an old mill."

"Oh, I see! The house at Cheltonwood. (Funny how it got that name. It isn't even in the village!) Well, let's see, I suppose the thing is, you're interested in one of the girls. Jay, the pretty one. I shouldn't, if I were you, laddie!"

His eyebrows arose and his face went cold. "I hope I never forget I'm a married man," he said, but Aunt Nerys permitted herself a wicked chuckle, and said, "No, dear boy, you behave in a very circumspect way, I allow, but in any case, she's taken. Even the other girl, the plain one, is being haggled over by two well heeled tradesmen. What's your worry?"

He was very good at keeping a poker face and disappointed her, but he wondered at himself for caring so much that Carlotta Buckland was referred to in such a way, and that it was generally known. Why *was* he worrying?

"I just want to know what's going to be got out of it," he said, woodenly. "And don't recommend me to ask Isolde, Aunt Nerys."

"Well, I suppose there's no harm in telling you. Something with water, d'you see, because they're floating in it. Awash, in that valley. Can't build on the place. Not stable enough. No industry could manage there. So — sink the place under water, make a whacking big lake, and a holiday camp all round with water sports. Local tradesmen will be very pleased with us. Well, whatever's the matter, Maxstead? You look quite horrified!"

As he didn't answer, she continued, "They might even keep the mill as an added attraction, though I doubt it. A bit ramshackle. Puff of wind and the whole thing'd go over. Oh, I must go — there's that husband of mine. If he gets into the library with a supply of brandy and cigars I'll never get him home."

Maxstead found Tim later, supervising a new supply of drinks coming up. "Tim, did you know what the mill was wanted for?"

He saw at once by the change in Tim's face, that he had.

"And you're not horrified?"

Tim shrugged. "I suppose I'm selfish. I only see that Jay can do her dressmaking anywhere, until she can get to Paris. As soon as I can afford it, if I ever can, I shall ask her to marry me, though I doubt if she'll have me. She'd hate to live on this estate, with . . . " He just stopped in time, from adding, 'with Isolde around making life difficult.'

Maxstead spent the next hour on the terrace, trying to cool off before supper, when he would have to make an appearance at Isolde's side. He hadn't spoken to her privately yet, but she'd ask that loaded question soon, he was quite sure, and what was he going to say? That he had given the Bucklands notice to quit, or that he hadn't, and had no intention of doing so? Which way would help them best, if at all?

Isolde rustled out to him at that moment. She really looked magnificent, he had to concede it to her. True, she could afford to. She was very rich indeed, but there were few women who could wear a dress with the bodice sewn all over with rhinestones, and a heavy border of the stones near the hem and not look vulgar. She just looked as if she had found the world's most clever dress designer and had the money to pay him and the courage to wear his daring designs.

She came out to him and was disposed to look pleased with him. "I thought you might decide not to come after all, Maxstead," she murmured, and laid a possessive hand on his arm. "You look rather splendid tonight."

He inclined his head, but couldn't stop looking amused, though for her own purposes, she wouldn't let her face show how annoyed she was. "I won't tell you how you look, Isolde. I got here too late to get in before everyone else." Still, it was a compliment, in that it was different to what every one else had said.

"Now, the million-dollar question, and I don't have to ask it, do I?" she said, her mouth still smiling. "Did you or didn't you?"

He knew what she meant, only too well. But a sixth sense told him not to answer for a moment. It was extraordinary; he had the oddest sort of feeling that that girl, Carlotta

Buckland, was near. Almost as if she, too, wanted to hear what he would say. What an idiotic thing to think, he told himself.

But it wasn't. He heard one of the servants say to someone, "He's up there, miss, on the terrace. You really can't go. to him now! Could I take a message?" The man had gone out to fix one of the lights that lit the grounds and there was Carlotta. Clever girl not to have tackled the front door, and what had she said to get so far? Well, he supposed she'd only to murmur that she'd brought the required answer to the question regarding the property known as the house at Cheltonwood, that Lady Powley was waiting for, wouldn't she? He had the most extraordinary feeling that everyone knew about it except himself and the Bucklands; everyone must have known for weeks that Isolde was angling to pull off another money spinner. They must have known for ages that Isolde wanted to do something with that land. It was water-logged. It didn't bring business to the district. It was no use to anyone except the Bucklands . . .

And all the while he had been abroad, all this had been boiling up and he had had no idea.

Isolde said, "Max, you aren't listening. What are you looking down there for? And what were you in a huddle with old Aunt Nerys about?"

"She was making me au fait with what's been happening while I've been out of the country," he said wryly.

Isolde's eyes narrowed. "Just what does that mean?"

"People tell me you're getting hard up and need cash pretty soon so you are throwing those people out of their house. Is that true?"

"I think you've been away from me too long, Maxstead," Isolde said softly, and wondered what that wretched girl from The Mill House was doing down there at the bottom of the steps, staring up at them. She remembered that she had asked Tim — when she had first

40

heard that Carlotta Buckland had two local tradesmen scrapping over her, both wanting to marry her — what on earth they could see in a plain girl like her, who had no money at all, and Tim had hesitated, before saying, "We-ell, Lady Powley, you have to know her. She's got something that draws people to her."

One of the dangerous ones, Isolde thought. Let's show her who Maxstead belongs to, then, and she took his arm possessively and put her face up close to his. It didn't have to be a kiss from a wife, to show who owned him. Just a possessive touch, and she observed Carlotta move sharply away.

3

MAXSTEAD arrived at The Mill House at eight thirty the next morning. By then the sparkle of dew had almost vanished from the grass and the heat haze had drifted away from the meadows, but the droplets of water flung out by the mill-wheel contained ink-blue and scarlet as they reflected the myriad glows of blossoms growing near and above. Climbers clung to the walls above the water; roses scrambled for space among the many other growing things and, apart from the rioting sound of the birds and the moving water, there was no sound. No sound of a car; too early for farm vehicles and probably as good arable land was away, well away, from this water-logged beauty spot, they didn't hear those, either. No aircraft, no sound of lawn-mowers, nor the biting thrust of a voice like Isolde's, giving orders, finding fault with those being carried out. He was glad to be away from Powley Court. Tonight he would manage to find solitude somewhere. Last night had not been pleasant and this morning had been worse. He hadn't expected to see Isolde up so early.

He stood in the shadows, beneath the trees, one part of him drinking in all the beauty that Isolde wanted to destroy, the other part of him thinking over last night, remembering all that had happened since they had seen that girl below the steps. What had she wanted, he wondered? She had made a nice job of getting clean away before he could shake off Isolde's clinging presence. If for nothing else, he felt he had a good excuse to come here this morning, to find out if Carlotta Buckland was in any sort of trouble. And yet she had seemed such a capable person, he really could see no possibility of her ever needing the help of someone like himself.

Isolde had put him in the picture about how he looked; how he would appear to a girl like Carlotta. "You're still as arrogant, darling, as you ever were," Isolde had said.

"Arrogant!" He had been shocked, but he had seen his face, almost at once, in one of the many tall ornamental mirrors that surrounded the room, and if he wasn't arrogant, then he was withdrawn, a man who didn't find it easy to smile, mix-and-mingle, as Isolde called it. Isolde's idea of that was all very fine; she bore down on a person, a wide smile dazzling, preventing the person looking at once at her eyes, which were usually ice-cold, calculating, and while she talked brilliantly, having apparently found out what the person liked or did, she looked round for someone to pair him off with, and she could do that very well. There were no wallflowers at Isolde's gatherings; no person miserably on the edge with nobody to talk to. Isolde was the perfect hostess and he (she had told him last night) was the perfect husband of the perfect hostess: just right to stand by her side, looking elegant, good-looking, masculine and arrogant.

"And now you've come back to me," she had purred. "I was thinking about it only last night and wondering what had sparked off that last row, but that must be all forgotten now. We'll go abroad somewhere. It isn't good for a girl to lose a handsome husband like you, with no real reason to give her friends. Of course I told them a titillating story of why you had to go abroad and stay so long. They all think you were doing business for me."

He had let her talk and, when she had paused to smile up at him, he had pinned a smile to his face and said between his teeth, "I have not come back to you, Isolde. I said when I went away, that I never would, and that still holds. We can't go on. If ever a couple were incompatible, it's us." And he had looked down at her to see how she was taking it.

They had been strolling in from the terrace at the time. Isolde had pinned a smile to her face, too, and he supposed that people must think they really had patched up their differences and were together again. He dimly realised they made a handsome couple. People must envy them. They had so much money, so much of everything, it seemed. Except happiness.

"What a lot of rot you talk, darling," Isolde had said, in reply to that little speech of his. "You will stay with me, you know. You can't do without me. I'm the one with the money, remember? You have expensive tastes. I have it on the best authority that that account Uncle Joseph left to see you were never entirely dependent on me (touching thought!) has long since vanished. Now be a good boy and come back and I'll float you again. You know you can't do without money."

"You're right, of course," he heard himself softly concede, and wondered what she would say if she ever found out that he had discovered a talent for making money and that he had used that amount her dear old uncle had given him, to play with and multiply it. What for, he asked himself bitterly? Just to reassure himself that he wasn't dependent on Isolde? Or because he had hated it so much when he had once overheard one of her friends calling him a beastly adventurer? Or was it just the same love of money that Isolde had, which was making her now anxious to sell that water-logged panorama before his dazzled eyes, and make another fortune out of it? He didn't know and he suddenly wished he could wipe out the memory of last night for ever.

He had stayed with her. After saying, "Would you stop harrying the Bucklands, not sell the land and turn them out, if I came back to you?" She had promised. Convincingly, too. So he had stayed, believed her, accepted her word and stayed. He hated himself. In the morning, around six, he had turned over to find himself in her extravagantly draped Italian bedstead, with a sleepy Isolde beside him. She had opened her eyes and smiled at him but he kept thinking of the wicked smile of a pretty kitten. "Did I promise something last night, darling?" she had murmured.

"You did," he had said slowly. "That you wouldn't proceed with the sale of the land, or turn out the family from the house at Cheltonwood."

Her eyes had widened. "I did that?" she had asked, in mock amazement. "You surely didn't believe me?"

Rage swept over him now, as he remembered her face. So innocent, so mischievous, as if that promise and the result of its not being kept were so much fun, and not to be taken seriously.

"Yes. I keep my promises. I expect you to keep yours."

"Oh, but I do! That is, if I mean them. I must have been a little drunk last night, to have made that promise, though. Anyway, whatever I was, I've changed my mind." And seeing his look of thunder, she lost her temper and flared, "Oh, be reasonable, Maxstead! Even Uncle Joseph wouldn't have agreed to keep that land lying idle just because of one ramshackle house on it and one ramshackle family in it, when it could be turned over to make an enormous sum and good business — good business and work for hundreds and a holiday place! You must be out of your mind if you think Uncle Joseph would have approved of letting such a scheme go to waste."

Well, she had said he was arrogant, and silent, ill tempered, and a lot of other things, and she had cried and stormed and bothered him while he was trying to get dressed, knowing that he was going to leave her. She knew, too, that if he went this time he wouldn't come back.

He had forgotten that if someone else took something away from Isolde, she at once decided she wanted it, even if she hadn't bothered about it before. So now he was removing himself from her life, she madly wanted to keep him. He had forgotten that. He felt a chill as he stood staring at the way the house was changing in the early sunshine, as the sun rose higher in the sky and new shapes were given to the tree shadows. To his delight a crimson-and-green kingfisher flashed out of a still pool that had at some time broken away from the tumbling turbulent waters. "Beautiful," he murmured, hardly aware that he had said it aloud.

"Yes, isn't it?" a young voice said, from somewhere below him, making him jump. He looked down to find a very small girl beside him. She had the tumbling dark short curls of Carlotta, the thin whiplash body of the boy — Stephen — and the beautiful face of the redhead Jay.

"You must be Holly," he murmured.

"Yes, how did you know, because I wasn't around when you came last night? Well, it stands to reason you are the mystery man who came because you're just like Carly described you to me."

"And how was that? Tell me," he urged.

A small brown hand slid into his and did strange things to him. He hadn't ever had the experience of a small friendly child's touch before. The young ones he had encountered in his world were mainly precocious, unfriendly and certainly not prone to slide a hand into his. Warmth, that was it. That was what this family had. He sensed it last night, the minute he had seen them all. Even the old uncle, furious as he was, had warmth in his very protection of his little family.

Holly thought for a moment, then repeated from memory, "Very big and dark and handsome and . . . remote, I think was the word she used, but I'm not quite sure what she meant and she was too busy to stop and explain. Actually she said 'another time, love' and that means she's not going to. Oh, well, grown-ups! And to think I shall be one, some day!"

He chuckled. "And a very handsome grown-up, you'll make, too, Miss Laura Hollington Buckland," he said, sweeping her a bow.

"Oh, do you really think so?"

"I am sure of it," he said gravely. "By the way, your sister more or less gave me permission to come this morning to see the place. I am not trespassing, you know," and he nodded at a tipsy trespass board leaning half against a tree in a little copse.

"Oh, no, I knew you were coming because Carly said, 'He'll be here, probably at cock-crow', so I got up early special. You're late."

She was a little puzzled at his snort of laughter. He could just imagine Carlotta glumly assuming he'd be over as early as it was light.

"Well, I'll show you around, and then we'll find some breakfast. I could do with some more."

"I haven't had any," he marvelled, and realised he was hungry.

"Well, the staff don't like serving it early, do they? That's what Jay's friend Richard says. I'm not quite sure how he knows what goes on at Powley Court, but he tells us very funny stories."

'Jay's friend Richard'. That Tim!

Does he now, Max thought! "What sort of stories? I like hearing funny ones," he murmured.

Holly said, "Well, about one time when the master came home from abroad somewhere and wanted a drink so he rang for it but the butler had his night off and he'd had a row with the housekeeper and she said nobody else was to do his job and the master could get it for himself anyway, and in the end it was the boot-boy who came up to get it. What's a boot-boy?"

So that's what had happened! Isolde, for all her money and domineering ways, couldn't control that great inflated domestic staff of hers! And, he thought, his skin growing hot with anger and embarrassment, they apparently thought little of him, to talk of him like that.

Well, what did he expect? Everyone knew Powley Court belonged to Isolde's family. Hadn't she given him the very first slap-down when she had kept her own name after marriage, graciously consenting to have the 'Jefferson' bit tacked on in front with a hyphen, knowing perfectly well nobody would bother to use it. Who called her Lady Jefferson-Powley now? Nobody! She had been Lady Powley before marriage and had remained so. He supposed that that had been part of the cause of the confusion here. If Carlotta wasn't interested in the family, she surely wouldn't have bothered to sort that out.

Holly required an answer, though, although she was busily showing him around as she did so. So while she showed him the kitchen garden, which she obviously considered very important, and her own special hideaway that had once been a gazebo but had partly collapsed and was supposed to be out of bounds because it was unsafe, he said, "I've only met one boot-boy in my life. A friendly soul. The very lowest in a very large staff of servants, and only anxious to please and be left alone." The very same boot-boy whose exploits Tim had apparently regaled the Buckland family with.

Holly said, "Look in there!" and he found he was staring into a large sunlit room with a table down the middle and all the walls covered in sensible shelving and cupboards. The nicest most livable kitchen he had ever seen, and Carlotta, unhurried, was making breakfast for all those lucky people. She worked with a rhythm, as if her mind was at peace, and yet it couldn't be, with all those burdens on her young shoulders. He couldn't take his eyes away from her.

"Come on, that's only our Carly. You've met her. Come and meet Don. He comes to work very early so he can have breakfast here. His old mother's a rotten cook. Don Foxwell, *you* know. He's the one who builds bits on to our house. He's always here. He thinks he's going to marry our Carly."

"And isn't he?" He badly wanted to know, though he kept telling himself it was no business of his.

Holly giggled. "Well, Keith Anscombe thinks he's going to, and we think it's fun. Like a puzzle, never knowing."

She showed him a sort of outhouse with a north light instead of a roof and she said proudly, "It isn't part of a glasshouse. It's the studio. Our mother used to paint there. Carly . . . " But she broke off and didn't finish what she had been going to say. "Come on, let's see if our Steve's caught any fish for lunch. I bet you didn't know this was full of fish. Nobody does."

He doubted that and wondered who owned the fishing rights. Steve, looking very unpleased to see him, tried to hide several large fish on the bank beside him.

"Good-morning, Steve," Max said genially. "I think, if I'm asked, I will stay to breakfast."

"These are for lunch," Steve said in an unfriendly voice.

"Not all of them," Holly corrected innocently. "Steve sells some to the fish-shop in the village, don't you, Steve? We sell everything we can't eat."

Steve directed a look of loathing at his sister but Max pretended not to see. "Jolly good idea," he commented, and to Holly, "Could I see the piano in the parlour again? I only glanced at it last night."

"The parlour's locked, I'm afraid, sir," Steve said, getting up and gathering his things together. The 'sir' made Max feel unaccountably old. "And if I may say so, my sister Carlotta was wanting a word with you. This way." And to his little sister, "Uncle's wanting you, Holly, *at once.*"

Carly was alone in the kitchen. The plates and cups were stacked to show mute evidence of the rest of the family having breakfasted well but with no waste of time. Where were they all?

He counted rapidly and realised that only two were missing, apart from the uncle: Jay and Amy.

"Good-morning," Max said to Carlotta, and felt a rush of genuine pleasure at being able to greet her again so soon. Last night he had felt miserably sure he would never see her again. Last night . . .

He brushed the memory back into the dark places of his mind, with all the other miserable memories, and watched Carlotta's face become wreathed in smiles she couldn't help. He was amazed. He thought she would be very cold with him.

"I'm sorry about last night," she said quickly. "I thought it would be such a good idea if I cycled over to Powley Court to try and see Lady Powley personally. I didn't know there was a big party on. Or that you were to be a guest there. I made myself scarce. It was a mad idea anyway, and Uncle Fergus was livid. I really shouldn't make him angry. It isn't good for him."

She pointed to a chair. "Would you like some breakfast?"

He nodded, rearranging his thoughts. So Carlotta hadn't guessed they were man and wife, he and Isolde! He should tell her, he supposed, but that wouldn't do. She would at once realise he had no influence there and he flinched from her knowing that. He would rate as the enemy; unbearable!

She deftly served up sausages, tomato slices, fried bread, bacon and two kidneys. "That enough? You have the look of a famished man."

This was what was served up at the Court, only one did it one's self at the sideboard, after investigating everything under the silver dish covers. Somehow it wasn't to be compared with this. He tucked in.

Carlotta poured tea for him and for herself and sat down facing him to stir sugar into hers and regard him thoughtfully. "Last night I was stunned at the thought of leaving here. Then I was angry. Then I had a number of good ideas, to put as counter-proposals, all of which I have since realised were pretty stupid. Lady Powley just wants to sell this land, I was told."

"Who told you that? Someone at Powley Court, you mean?" he asked carefully. He really wanted to know.

"Yes. I was leaving, pretty quickly, mad at myself for coming, and I couldn't find my bike. Someone had moved it. By the time I did find it, this other chap came out and told me it was no use trying to see Lady Powley. She was adamant." She paused. "I think he must have been her secretary. Perhaps he was scared she'd be livid with him for letting someone get so near to her, to question her plans."

"What did the man look like, Carly?" He didn't intend to use the little name her family had used, and he was about to apologise, when he saw she was pink faced, smiling broadly. "That sounded nice," she told him.

"I'm Max," he said. It felt, just then, that they had grasped hands, across the table, hers with the warmth of young Holly. Yet they hadn't moved. Just quietly exchanged their 'little' names. And it shouldn't be, he told himself wretchedly.

Carly knew nothing of the turmoil within him. She was thinking of a word picture to fit the man who had spoken to her. "A dapper little rat-faced man, carefully dressed and pressed, his hair slicked down, very anxious expression, very neat way of speaking, so I must understand in case I was an idiot."

Max snorted with smothered laughter. That was Winters, Isolde's new solicitor. But had he been there at the party? And why? "You must be an artist, to paint such a word picture, to even notice such details. I know who you mean. He's a solicitor, actually."

"Yes, I'm an artist," she said, her laughter gone again. Now she looked ravaged. What hidden nerve had he jangled by a careless word?

He was at once deeply contrite. "Have I said something?" and then he remembered someone had said her mother had been an artist. Now he didn't know what to say, since her mother had died fairly recently. Or had she? He tried to work out dates and times, but all he could remember was that the father had been their last bereavement and that was a year ago.

She shook her head, as if to clear it. "Sorry. I'm a bit edgy on that subject, I'm afraid. I just like . . . sketching. That's all."

She tried to dismiss it, lightly, but he knew it wasn't so easily dismissed. Little Holly had started to say something about Carly when she had shown him the 'studio' and had hastily backed away from the subject before she had got too involved. And the boy, Stephen, had looked rather odd about Carly, come to think of it.

"Look," he said, "I feel it's gone all wrong. This wasn't how I wanted it. I've blundered in here, upset your uncle . . . "

She sobered again. "Yes, you did,

didn't you? Funny, I've never seen him like that before, on meeting a new person. Oh, but you have met him before, haven't you? No, your grandfather knew his father, and so he knew of you. Complicated, isn't it? Still, why should he . . . "

"Yes why should he?" Max murmured, staring at the wall behind her. "Perhaps he doesn't like the younger generation to spend so long abroad as I have. Perhaps he feels I should have stayed home . . . on the land . . . "

"Oh, yes, that must be it!" she said, relief lighting her face. The smile was back. "Yes, that's a big thing with Uncle Fergus. Duty to one's job, or heritage, as the case may be. Oh, well, that's settled that point." She wanted it settled, he could see. But it didn't settle anything.

"But I feel nobody likes me here and I want you all to like me," he said.

"Why do you? I like you," she assured him.

"Even though I came with the bad

news?" he probed gently.

"Oh, that. Yes, it's a problem," she said, yet oddly he felt that she wasn't all that concerned about the place. He didn't understand that.

"I can't let them uproot you all," he said with sudden passion. "I must do something about it, I simply must!"

"What can you do?" she asked. "Let me see, if you're not Tim Roberts, as I'd thought at first, then you're not the agent, so just what do you do in connection with Powley Court? I don't think I understand."

"Didn't your uncle tell you?"

"No. You mean he knows?"

"Yes, and I'd rather tell you myself, than have someone else tell you," he said, drawing a deep breath to say, 'I'm Lady Powley's husband'. It would have cleared so many things up, but at the same time she would have stopped liking him and he didn't want that. He couldn't bear the thought of not being able to talk to this girl, watch the play of emotions on that lovely face of hers, the clear eyes looking straight at his. Who was it said she was plain? Plain! Oh, Isolde! Well, she would, of course. Carlotta wasn't pretty, but she had an innate charm and strong personality that did away with the need of mere prettiness. She was . . . what? Not like any woman he'd met before? That was the most trite thing he could think of. A knife turned in his heart as he thought that it was too late to think things like that. Finished his marriage might be, but he still wasn't free. But there was no reason why he shouldn't help these people, was there?

The four words never slid off his tongue after all, for Holly tumbled into the room. "Quick, quick, Carly!" she choked, trying to get her breath. "It's Amy! She was reaching for the kitten and . . . she fell in the mill-stream!"

4

THEIR chairs fell over with twin crashes, as both he and Carly leapt up. "No!" Max said to Carly. "I'll do it — I'm a strong swimmer," and he rushed out of the room behind little Holly, who was sobbing as she went.

Max tore off his jacket as he ran. He had some idea of what the water would be like but fear tore at his throat as he got near and heard the noise. Would they be in time?

Carly was close on his heels and then his impression of what happened was confused because everything seemed to happen at once. The boy, Stephen, was manoeuvring a stout pole across for Amy to hang on to. Someone else had thrown a rope but now she had lost it, her hands slipping, so that she could hardly grasp Steve's pole. The water was tugging at the child and her strength was failing.

And then another hazard presented itself. Jay appeared from another direction and shouted to Steve, "Get back, you idiot! You can't swim!" It was the worst possible thing to do. Carly's despairing face lived in Max's mind as he hit the water, for Jay's shout had broken Steve's concentration and he let go of the pole.

Max reached out, heart in his mouth, and literally plucked at Amy as it seemed she would be sucked in against the great wheel. He remembered a wave of anger against everyone for allowing the mill-wheel to run, in a family house. He was a strong swimmer and his rage gave him strength, but this needed a phenomenal effort and it struck him he might not be able to make it. It was as if an army of hands were pulling him and the child back to the wheel. Time seemed to stand still, yet it was only seconds, and then Steve got his pole across again. It missed the brick he had

had it wedged into, so he shoved it into the depths and managed to make it stay for Amy to hold on to. It helped Max while he gathered strength to push her to the water's edge, where they were all waiting to grab her. And then, as he was hauling himself up to the bank with the help of the boat-hook Carly had found and thrust towards him, he saw the dog come bounding. The uncle, attracted by the shouting and noise, had come out and forgotten to hold the dog back. It looked as if it were going to gambol up to them, just behind little Holly. She would be pushed in and she was such a tiny scrap! It was all he could think of. He stopped concentrating on holding the boat-hook and threw his arms up to point, shouting at the others. At the same time something hit him on the head and he blacked out.

He came to in bed. A strange bed. His head was throbbing and the light was too strong, and he felt he should know the young man who was sitting beside him, a cool hand on his pulse. But the bedroom worried him. He'd seen it before and knew he oughtn't to be here.

Then he saw Carly, coming in with a bowl of something steaming hot, set on an attractive little tray with a spoon beside it. And this . . . this was her late parents' room and he had been put in here . . .

He tried to get up but his head felt as if it would burst. Carly said amiably, "You'll be in terrible shape if you don't keep still, Max. Your head hit one of the pieces of flint from uncle's rockery. It must have fallen in at that moment, because we were all tramping round it."

His anger returned. "There's going to be more trouble. You know that, don't you? Idiot business, keeping the wheel turning, with small children and animals!" He was thinking it might be as well if the Bucklands were forced to leave this place, and it seemed she read his thoughts accurately.

"It's all right," she said. "Uncle's stopped the wheel. The place will flood a bit but what's it matter? This is Dr Guy Morrison."

Maxstead tried to think. "Morrison? Should I know you? Sorry, but I have a sledgehammer thudding in my head."

"Well, we'll talk a bit later," Dr Morrison said, turning him over to Carly's tender mercies. "I want to see your uncle," he told her. "I'll come back and have a word with this chap afterwards," and, nodding, he took himself to Fergus Buckland's room. Obviously no stranger here, Max thought.

"You might have been killed," Carly said severely.

"What did you expect me to do? Jump about on the bank and shout good advice to that poor child?"

"Oh, no, I suppose not," she said, wiping her forehead with a tired hand. "I'm glad I'm home all the time now and can keep an eye on things, though."

"Aren't you usually at home all the

time?" he asked quickly.

She frowned, as if angry at having said that. "No, but I am now. Drink this good home-made soup. Vegetables we grow ourselves, puréed by pushing the stuff through a sieve. None of your fantastic electric gadgets in this place." She grinned. "If we so much as plugged in an iron, the generator would give up and die."

"You mean you don't even have an electric iron?" He couldn't believe it.

"Well, no, one of the blessings of being hard up in this place is that there's always a fire going in the solid-fuel stove, so we do everything from it. Even baths."

"Oh, no, I don't believe that!"

"We're floating in stuff that's crying to be burned on that stove so we don't have to buy coal, and the lamps are pumped up and take very little fuel. Friends of mine are always calling in electric repair men, but we have none of those problems. Oh, you should really try it!"

"I am trying very hard to keep you pinned down to the one subject, Carlotta Buckland," he said severely. "You slide away into different conversational channels. Of course, it may be a polite way of saying that what I wanted to know was no concern of mine . . . "

"Oh, no, I didn't mean to." Now she was distressed, and either accidentally misconstrued what he wanted to know, or did it deliberately. He suspected the latter, though how could he grumble, since he wasn't being open with her as to his own identity? She said frankly, "The generator is really very old, and it's run by water power, and of course if we stop the wheel, there is no other way of working the generator."

He gave up and closed his eyes. He'd forgotten what he wanted to know. Oh, yes, the highly interesting comment that she was only at home at the weekend. Then where else did she go?

Carly thought his head was paining him, so she took advantage of his closed eyes to take the tray and creep out.

He was on the verge of sleep when the doctor came back and sat down beside him.

"You'll live, you know," he said, a small smile turning up the corner of his mouth. It was a thin face, a rather likeable face. "The thing is, I'm in a bit of a spot, aren't I? Well, Lady Powley and the Powley Court doctor between them will make mincemeat of me, for stealing their patient."

"I'm not anybody's patient. Sir Norbert is Isolde's physician, and for goodness' sake don't let them know who I am, here."

"Fergus Buckland has already told me that for some reason you are pretending to be the agent. May I know the reason?"

Max was exasperated. "You make it sound as if I were trying to deceive everyone. How could I, in a place like this, even if I wanted to? The thing is, a very natural mistake was made, when I turned up with Tim Roberts in the car. You know Tim Roberts?"

The doctor nodded. "Nice chap, but foolish. Playing some silly game, I hear, about being a mysterious 'Richard' for young Jay's benefit. She won't forgive him when she finds out, you know, and she surely will, in a place like Cheltonwood."

"Yes, well, I was going to tell Carlotta who I was, but got interrupted by the accident this morning. I think she must know who I am! Why, she turned up at Powley Court last night, and saw me with Isolde."

"What on earth did she go there for?" the doctor gasped.

"Wild idea of begging Isolde not to turn them out of here."

"Oh, help!" The doctor rubbed his forehead. "Someone should tell her that a better bet would be to show every desire to be turned out. (Oh, sorry — shouldn't have said that!) But it's true, isn't it?" he said, pulling a face, and Max nodded wearily.

"I've been abroad for ages. All this is news to me, really," Max frowned.

"I was trying to get to know the family better, to see if I could do something for them," he admitted. "Well, you may not have been told, but the uncle's old man and my grandfather were buddies."

"I've been told, just now," Guy Morrison said.

"I gather Fergus is a tiny bit miffed at my second appearance here."

The doctor studied his nails, then finally said, "The thing is, Fergus wants to see Carly and Jay happily married. There's been enough heartbreak in this family as it is."

"What makes you think my presence will add to it?" Max asked tartly. "I merely came back to this country to ... settle my affairs, before going abroad again."

"That isn't what Cheltonwood is saying." The doctor looked at him. "It really isn't any use exploding and saying your affairs are no-one else's business, because Cheltonwood has nothing else to do but speculate on other people's business and word is going around that you have gone back to your wife." He raised his brows as Max's face flushed. "Keep your cool, my friend, if you want to be up out of this bed in a day or two. The thing is, Cheltonwood wants the project that is suggested. A beauty spot such as this is no use to them. You can't see it from the road so it won't bring tourists. Cheltonwood itself is cut off from everything by the new by-pass. There's high unemployment, practically no local social amenities and such a poor bus service, that people in the place are literally cut off with no hope. Don't tell me what the date is," he smiled at a new burst of indignation from Max. "As you say, you've been out of the country too long. There are many places in this country of ours, just as badly off as Cheltonwood." He patiently put it into other words. "The project will bring trade, employment, the lot."

"Good heavens, can't something else be thought up for them, without turning the Bucklands out of their home? Do they have to be the lambs to the slaughter?"

"I think it sounds as if Fergus was right and you have a personal interest," Guy Morrison said severely.

"If I weren't laid low, I'd knock your block off for talking to me like that, and we've only just met," Max growled, but his mouth was twitching at the corners. He found he rather liked the Buckland's G. P. "All right, so I've a personal interest — I like the family. I've never met such a delightful bunch of people before. Tell me, why does Carly only come home at week-ends? I gathered she didn't want to tell me, nor would she disclose why she looked so unhappy when I asked if she was an artist?"

"What else has she told you? The two things are tied up, you see. Has she mentioned her father?"

"Yes, the chap who built a new room on, every time a new child appeared so I gathered."

Dr Morrison sighed. "She feels bad

about her — well, not dislike, but impatience with — her late father, so she builds him up, to strangers. He was a charming man. My father had the practice then. We've sort of grown up with the Buckland family. Believe me, Carly's father never did anything practical. Oh, yes, once — he had a modest win on a horse, and after that he was sure he'd win the family a fortune, and proceeded to ruin them. That was why most of them had outlandish names — the names of the horses he lost on. But Carly's mother was way out, there — it didn't shame him. He just took it in his stride, so she did her poor bit to bring in some money. She was a commercial artist, with not enough time or privacy to do the job properly. She worked herself into the ground."

"Yes, I think I've been told some of that, here and there. But what I want to know is — "

"About Carly," Dr Morrison said, without approval. "She really has great talent, but no money for training. No, her father didn't send her to a decent school. He didn't do that for any of them. So she tried for a scholarship herself, but she had to work to get the money, and she had no training, so she got a weekday job, going to classes when she wasn't working in the hotel, and she'd come home at week-ends to run things here. I put my foot down. I could see she was going the same way as her mother."

"What about the uncle? Has he no money?"

"Poor chap, he works all the time, writing, to support the family. They grow things and sell what they don't consume. They all work, to their capacity, but it's never enough. And Carly won't forgive me for making her come back."

And you mind that very much, Max thought, with a twinge of real pain at the thought of some other man having the freedom, the right, to care for Carlotta Buckland. He closed his eyes.

The doctor got up. "I don't know what I'm going to do about you. If there's a fuss, assure them all at Powley Court that I don't want you as a patient. I was only coming in for a routine visit to Fergus anyway. Lucky I came just then, or you'd have been in a spot. Imagine having to get Sir Norbert over here to patch you up." He grinned unfeelingly. "That's what happens to people who start pretending. Remember what Shakespeare had to say about the tangled web we weave."

Max grinned, totally unrepentent. "I shall be leaving the country soon, so don't worry," but he wasn't feeling so light-hearted about it. "Before you go, have you got any idea about what could be done to thwart this project business?"

"Who wants to thwart it? Not I. Not Cheltonwood, to a man. Not anyone, so far as I know."

"The Buckland family?" Max frowned.

"Make sure first that it's what they want, too," Guy Morrison said, as he went to the door. "If they haven't actually said they mind leaving here, I'd think first, if you are considering throwing a spanner into the works. In any case, Lady Powley will soon find some other way of making money out of the land. She's been wanting to get rid of it for ages."

"Has she?" Max asked, startled, then glowered to think he knew so little of what his wife wanted. But it followed, of course. She'd want the money, as if she wasn't rolling in the stuff already.

The door shut on the doctor. Max liked him as a man, but hated him as someone who was in love with Carly. And was he right, about the project?

5

"RICHARD'S here," Carly said, when she brought him his light evening meal. "Jay's over the moon. I like Richard, but . . . I wish Jay didn't."

Guy Morrison had been back to look at him and said he could get up the next day but sit about and take it easy. "And no more rescues. Let the little blighters look after themselves. They did it very well before you turned up."

One more day. Maxstead found himself wishing he could stay here for a week, a month even. The only thing he was glad about was that he hadn't let Isolde know where he was staying and hadn't moved back to Powley Court. He shuddered as he remembered the night of the party.

"Why," he asked Carly, firmly, "why do you wish Jay didn't like him?"

"Well, he's charming. But we can't find out anything about him. It may be an old-fashioned idea but I want my sister to marry the man she is so dotty about, and we should be told what his background is, all about him, whether he's got enough money to marry her."

Max's heart went out to her. Poor Carly was praying Jay's boyfriend wouldn't turn out to be like her father.

If only Tim hadn't been an idiot and called himself Richard, he, Max, could have reassured Carly. Well, it would surely have helped to have said they'd been at school together, stayed at each other's homes in the holidays' wouldn't it? She would have been reassured to know that Tim was the youngest of five and that although there hadn't been enough cash to buy him a place on the board of some company, at least his father was a professional man and the family wasn't poor! But he couldn't have said anything about Tim, could he, not only because of his idiotic guise of the mythical 'Richard' but because Carly would naturally want to know more about Max's background.

His and Carly's thoughts must have run parallel, for she suddenly said, "If only his grandfather had been a friend of Uncle Fergus's father, like yours was! Now that's a good solid recommendation."

"Is it?" he asked, real yearning in his voice.

"Yes, it is. Yes, it really is, except . . . well, Uncle Fergus won't speak about it. Did the families have a row or something? You tell me about it, Max."

"Why do you want to know? I daresay the two old gentlemen were always having rows. I don't remember much about my grandfather, anyway."

"What do you do for a living?" she shot at him. Well, it was bound to happen, wasn't it? Well, since she didn't know who he was, why didn't he tell her the truth? It would give him a real pleasure to tell someone. So far nobody knew.

"I had a certain sum in the bank and it wasn't going to take me very far, so I decided I'd show everyone how wrong they were about my business abilities, so I made it work for me. It's . . . a great deal bigger now."

"Yes, but what do you *do*?" she insisted.

"I can't admit to doing anything respectable, like being a doctor," he said deliberately, and watched her face.

"Oh, like Guy! He's a dear! We've known him all our lives," she said, but he couldn't feel that she was in love with the doctor, unless she had schooled her face to give nothing away. "So you're not a doctor, Max. I do believe I guessed that. So what are you? Is it a secret?"

"No, I loathe secrets. I'll tell you, but I can assure you, you won't think it very thrilling. I'm a businessman. That is, if I come across, say, a little firm, with a few people struggling to stop it going bankrupt, I buy it up, feed new life into it, and when it's thriving, I sell it at a much higher price than I gave for it. That's being a businessman.

"Oh. Is it?" she said blankly, plainly disappointed.

"Yes. It is," he smiled, and absently took her hand. She seemed to get more out of the touch of his hand than the story of his business life. But he had to show her what that business life meant. "It does entail having a bit of a flair, you know," he urged. "I mean, I don't just buy up any old firm, which might be due to die on me anyway and leave me the poorer. No, it means having a sort of sixth sense, if you like. Oh, it's hard to explain. I'm in love with the small business, giving the small chap a boost. I get lots of ideas."

"Tell me," she said, rather dreamily, but she was only looking at his face, not taking in what he said about his work. He decided to shock her into listening, by taking a personal example. The personal angle always made people listen.

"Well, that little picture on the

dressing-table, for example."

She went all frosty, at once. "What about it?" she asked coldly.

"I imagine it is hand-painted. It is doomed to stay for ever, unseen, in a bedroom in The Mill House."

"*Doomed?*"

"Oh, dear, I've said the wrong thing. Well, what I mean is, whoever did it has a delicate charm and a lot of talent, and I could make a great deal of money out of that if the person would do some more."

"How?" she asked guardedly. "It's just a picture of a cottage, with a little boy and a dog."

"Yes, but he's rather a cute little boy, rather like a pixie. The dog's got a cute face too. Now, I see that couple in different clothes, different country places — perhaps a different cottage in each study — and I could make a packet by calling them a name, say, 'Jack and Mack', and marketing them." He smiled and nodded encouragingly, but she still didn't see.

"Marketing them? I don't think I understand."

"My dear, have you never seen a favourite character, a story-book sort of character, popping up on mugs and baby plates, towels, children's pinafores and shirts, even on kids' toothbrushes? On the tops of notepaper, calendars, oh, the lot! Surely!"

"Oh, that. That's what advertising agencies do." She sounded disgusted.

"You've met them? Well, my dear, I have an advertising agency. I rescued it when it was going down the drain and now it's mine, but even they are glad of ideas and artists' work at times," he said dryly. "By the way, this is all very secret — people think I'm a character who never has two pence to rub together so don't let on that I'm not hard up any more, will you?" So that Isolde won't find out, he added anxiously to himself. He had forgotten that angle.

But of course, to keep such a thing secret took away the authenticity of it in Carly's eyes. "I don't believe you've done all this captain-of-industry stuff," she said quietly, getting up.

"I know you don't," he agreed and let it go at that. "By the way, you didn't seem very upset at the idea of Lady Powley turning you all out of this house. Am I right?"

She looked hunted for a moment. Then she said, "What do you care? When Guy Morrison discharges you, probably tomorrow, you'll go back to wherever you came from, and we shall never see you again. I don't know why you came here at first, really I don't. I can't believe Lady Powley told you to do the job. It's the work of her agent. (I really must get to meet this Tim Roberts!) The thing is, being away from the place most of the week. The week-ends never seemed to have anything happening, and nobody else was working, in case you're wondering why I've never met him!"

"Well, I've met him. I know him well. He's a very nice chap." He smiled wryly, and added, "But it wouldn't make any difference if you did meet him because you wouldn't believe a word he said. You don't, do you?" He shrugged, "You don't believe a word I say, either."

"No, but that's because I get the impression . . . oh, I don't know. I feel that you're putting up a front. I didn't at first. I think it was when you spoke to Uncle Fergus. He doesn't like you. You know that, don't you? And it's positively the first time that Uncle Fergus has disliked a person I have liked."

"You put that in the past tense. You mean you did like me and now you've gone off me?"

She didn't want to answer that, but she drove herself to. "Yes, I think that's true. It's since you told me all this rigmarole about being rich and a businessman and small companies and making money out of that!" and she pointed to the little picture. "I did that, and I know my own limitations.

I put it there because . . . well, nobody touches anything in this room, and it was a sort of salute to my mother, who was a good artist. But to say you can make big money out of it . . . no, that's going too far and it's ruined everything."

"I wish you didn't disbelieve me, Carlotta, honestly. What's wrong with me having a talent for business and making money?"

"Uncle Fergus said . . . I have to say it. He said you were good-for-nothing. Oh, I know you dress expensively and have a smart car, but what does that indicate? Not necessarily that you are clever at making big money yourself and Uncle Fergus is angry about you all the time. Well, he's a good judge of character, and it seems I'm not. I'm sorry, Max, but it's all . . . spoiled . . . somehow. I'm so grateful to you for saving Amy this morning, but you've ruined . . . something rather nice that just came into my life."

When Carlotta terminated a conversation, it was terminated. He could see that and he wasn't at all pleased, for she hadn't answered the one question he so badly wanted an answer to: had he been mistaken, or hadn't they really minded at the thought of being forced to leave the house at Cheltonwood?

Max returned to his hotel and checked out. He was quite sure Isolde was aware of which hotel he was staying in, and at this stage it was imperative that he should not be somewhere where she could call on him at a moment's notice. He couldn't think what had changed Isolde's mind about him. When he had left the country, she had made it plain that she was very glad to see him go. They had had a blazing row, which had upset him. Shouting matches were not his line: they were Isolde's. His was the icy and silent rage. He hated scenes, considering them degrading. Part of the trouble was that his silent anger had goaded Isolde, who didn't understand it, and she had laid a series of verbal traps until his anger had spilled over. That, for him, had been final, but Isolde could never allow someone else to terminate something. It had to be her. It could be that that was the reason she wanted him back again now. It wouldn't last; she would end it herself and that would really be final. But for Max it had ended long ago. He despised himself for thinking that she would come to an arrangement with him, in return for letting the Bucklands off the hook.

And so he shifted his base to a place where she would never think of finding him: the vacant flat above the offices of one of his companies, in Trowstock. Nearby Trowstock, where everybody went in to shop and to bank; the market town that wouldn't let itself be modernised. A place he didn't really like, but where it was natural that he should be seen.

It bothered him that Carlotta wouldn't believe him when he had tried to tell her how he had made good. Furious with himself, he had to admit that it was rather a boy's trick to try and spring that surprise just to hear her approbation. He had to admit it to himself: he was pleased with himself for having left what had always struck him as an adventurer's stance. Well, he had married Isolde for her money, hadn't he? Lots of chaps did it in his world, but he hadn't liked it and he had got himself out of it, and now he hadn't a penny of Isolde's money. Even the money her uncle had given him was still intact at the bank, though he had used it to make more. Was it a flaw in his character that he should mind so very much about this? He would have liked to think it indicated his independence, a thing Carlotta should have noticed and approved of. Instead, she had thought he was 'shooting a line' and that he wasn't rich at all. And what was he going to do now, about that delightful sketch she had made?

Carlotta solved that for him herself the next day. She sent it to him. He was astonished as he opened the package, delivered to his hotel just as he was moving out, to take up residence at the flat. With it was a brief note: "I'm sorry I got annoyed with you. I wish you hadn't pretended to be rich. Why didn't you just say you would like the sketch? I would have given it to you then. Well, I'm giving it to you now, because I would like to, but please don't pretend any more about being rich." And she had put the initial 'C' by way of signature.

He was astonished. He wanted to be pleased with the gift, but now there was a sting in the tail, and he must accept it as an unasked-for gift and he couldn't make use of it as he had wanted to.

Like Carlotta, he was hugely independent and chafed at being held down over something he wanted to do. Well, she had given him a surprise with this present: why shouldn't he give *her* a surprise by launching it?

Carlotta . . . His thoughts drifted towards her all the time. He couldn't stop thinking about her, yet he had known her such a little while. He could no more say what it was about her that appealed to him, than jump over the moon. She wasn't beautiful like Jay. She hadn't the winsome appeal that young Amy had. She wasn't cute, as Holly was. She couldn't be said to be compounded of the charm of the other three. No, she was just herself, but her personality was so strong, she made him forget every other woman. She made him even forget he was not free to dream about her, he told himself curtly. For some reason she had not caught on just who he was, but one day she would, and then what would happen? He flinched from the thought, but it was too late to do anything about it.

Fergus was worried, too. If only that wretched woman hadn't been greedy for the money the land would bring . . . but no, that wasn't right, he corrected himself. If the land had been his — and he had possessed the drive and business acumen that Lady Powley had — then he, too, would want to get rid of it. And he had to face it, the Mill House was not exactly the best place to bring up a young family.

And there was the question of his health. Sooner or later he would have to let that damned doctor ship him off to hospital. This couldn't be allowed to go on. He grinned to himself as he thought of Guy Morrison. So deceptively quiet, thin, *reasonable*, yet he wasn't any of those things. He was a fighter and had already been far too voluble on what he thought of Fergus's stupid holding back from getting himself cured while there was time. If an opportunity didn't crop up to slap him into a hospital bed, Fergus was pretty sure that Dr Morrison would make one.

He gloomily stared out of his window. He would have liked to think of Carlotta as Dr Morrison's wife. He guessed the doctor was keen on her. Carly married safely to a doctor, he thought, drumming on the window-sill, and the beautiful

Jay married to . . . who? That young chap who looked after Lady Powley's business? No, he didn't think Tim Roberts, likeable as he was, would be strong enough to hold Jay down.

Then there was the problem of Steve, who, at fourteen, was eating his heart out to go to horticultural college. Was he physically suitable for the land and did he realise what the marketing side of it entailed? But Steve had the ambition to design gardens for private customers. Where had he got that idea, Fergus wondered irritably. As for Amy and Holly, there were two more problems coming up. Both girls knew passionately what they wanted to do in life, even though young Holly was only six. She had inherited her grandmother's beautiful singing voice, but whereas her grandmother had been content to stay home and sing for concerts and private parties, Holly wanted a career. Some fool had visited her school and heard the infants singing and picked out with surprise and pleasure the cute child with the voice, and had said roundly that it should be developed, and Holly wasn't going to let go of that idea.

Money . . . money for their careers, money to put this house right, or, better still, to get out of it. He wondered if Lady Powley could be trusted to find them another house as she had apparently promised (or was it just the empty promise of that young man who couldn't take his eyes off Carly?) or would Lady Powley wash her hands of the whole affair? He had a grim fear that they would find themselves with the money to buy a house, basing it on the market value of The Mill House, which would be alarmingly low. And they would finish up in a town, in a street of identical houses, with no peace for his work or anything else, and no garden for Steve to work in and dream over. And what about that young man, Maxstead Jefferson? Clearly he hadn't told Carlotta that he was Lady Powley's husband, and for heaven's sake how come Carlotta didn't know? Well, did the others know either? But one day, someone they met outside would casually say something, and Carlotta would be so angry and feel so cheated. Fergus asked himself worriedly if it would not be better if he himself told her, quietly, reasonably? The trouble with Carly was that one couldn't be quiet and reasonable with her over an issue that meant a lot to her. Besides, they would probably be interrupted before he had finished what he wanted to say, leaving her with the wrong impression. But no, he must tell her. Suppose he was shipped off to hospital before he could see that she was made aware of that highly important fact?

In the event, it was Carly herself who stopped her uncle from saying what he had intended. He found her crying in her room. When Carlotta resorted to tears, he thought, embarrassed and anxious, then there must be something very wrong indeed. He said gently, "My dear child, whatever is it? Are you ill?"

Her crying had been silent, but deep. She had been shaking with that terrible silent grief and Fergus thought, she had found out. Found out in quite the wrong way.

"Carlotta, I am your friend, I hope, as well as your uncle and guardian," and she looked up sharply at his unusually firm tone. "What is the matter, child? I may be able to sweep the whole thing away for you." But as her whole face filled with doubt, he said desperately, "It's about that young man, isn't it? Maxstead Jefferson!" and the doubt went, and her face was flooded with relief.

"Oh, yes, yes, it is, but now I know, I don't mind so much," she said, shrugging a little, as she wondered if her uncle would really agree with her that a young man's boasting about riches he didn't possess was a serious flaw in his character. To Carly it was a very big flaw and it worried her. "I'll admit that at first, when I first discovered it, I thought I'd never come to terms with it," she said, half to herself. "But now I've had time to think about it, well, it seems to be being done everywhere. I shall have to accept it, I suppose.',

"Accept it?" Her uncle sounded as stunned as he felt. He was sure she meant that Maxstead had told her he was married. Well, girls did tend to go out with married men these days and think nothing of it, but not his beloved Carly, surely?

"He seemed rather surprised that I should make a fuss about it at first," she went on.

"Well, he would do!" Fergus said grimly. "But are you sure you're right in accepting it? Don't you feel you might have difficulty in trusting him in other things?"

"Well, yes, but . . . I'm hoping that I shall find I don't mind so much later on. I mean, well, I might be just *thinking* he means so much to me, mightn't I? I don't know. I've never felt like this about a man before. I won't rush anything. I'll let it ride, and perhaps later I'll find it will fade, and that I was mistaken," but the listening Fergus heard the break in her voice and his own hopes for her future happiness plummeted to zero. "He's . . . he's a man who . . . somehow fills one's waking thoughts," she faltered.

"Yes, but think, child, only heartbreak can come out of this," Fergus urged. Not only because Maxstead was a married man but that he was the husband of Lady Powley, of all people.

"Yes, I thought of that," Carly allowed. "Well, I won't make a big fuss and cut the thing off. I'll let it ride. Just be friends, for a while. Let it die a natural death."

"Yes, do that," Fergus, slightly behind her, gasped, as a pain of greater magnitude than ever before ripped through his body, making it seem that he was being sliced in two. Carly heard the strangled breath with the words and leapt up.

"Uncle Fergus, you're ill! You're white as a sheet! Here, sit down and wait while I send someone for the doctor."

"The doctor, yes," Fergus gasped. Dr Morrison, his one hope for Carly's happy future. If he could persuade the doctor to consider Carly as his wife, it might be the answer to everything. Everything!

6

THIS attack had been sharper, but Fergus recovered from it more quickly than usual and as the consultant who was considered by Dr Morrison to be the best man at their disposal for Fergus's treatment was away on holiday just then, Fergus didn't get sent to hospital. "But no more getting excited about this family of yours," Dr Morrison said firmly.

"What sort of advice is that?" Fergus asked weakly, wondering how he could lead up to what he wanted to say. "If only there were someone else strong enough, capable enough, to take over."

"They don't need taking over," Dr Morrison said firmly. "They've got Carly in charge, and Jay isn't a child. Steve is a very sensible, mature sort of lad, and Amy and Holly will be no trouble. So will you stop your worrying?"

It had slid out of his reach again, that carefully laid lead towards asking the doctor what was really a delicate if worrying question. Nothing more was said about it. Fergus decided he'd better follow medical advice and rest and not get upset, and Maxstead didn't come to The Mill House for the next few days.

He had his own problems. On the face of it, he and Carly seemed to have quarrelled, and the way he had thought towards a reconciliation now didn't seem such a good idea. He should have remembered how things worked. He had taken the little picture to a friend of his and, before he could finish explaining that he wanted to launch it on the commercial market as a surprise for the young artist, his friend raved over it.

"Max, darling," she said, "you have a positive genius for finding a sure-fire winner in the most unlikely places! Where did this come from? Somebody's attic? Well, it's old-fashioned, but that should add to its charm," and before he could protest, she had brought in other people working on schemes for Max's commercial empire and the thing was well and truly out of his hands.

Now he must go and see Carly and tell her what he had done, and supposing she said she hadn't given permission to have it used, and didn't want it used? Money didn't seem to dazzle Carly, nor in fact anyone at The Mill House. Calmly and serenely they accepted they had little of it, and promptly pitted their brains and energies into finding the necessities of life without it, or with as little of the stuff as they could scrape up. They really were an extraordinary and delightful family, he found himself thinking, with tenderness. What Isolde would have thought if she could have seen into his mind just then, he shuddered to think.

Yet he was soon to know. He ran into her coming out of a little antique shop just off the High Street, the only local shop that Isolde admitted existed. She had a bundly parcel under her arm and was clearly about to drive herself home. "Max! I'm so glad I ran into you! Come to the car — I want you to be the first to see what I've got. A real find, and that fool just didn't know what it was worth!" she said, dismissing the antique dealer and all his staff.

It would be something in wrought iron, he guessed. Wrought ironwork appeared to be the fashion. But with the hunting season coming up, Isolde would soon turn her attention to buying up horses others of her kind were having to part with, owing to money troubles. Isolde's calendar was predictable, with the exception of the subject of The Mill House.

He went to her car with her and let her drive him out of the town. This, he thought, might be a good time to talk to her. How much more private could you get than in a woman's car, with no telephone interruptions, no servants to pop in and remind you of appointments to be kept. No, this must be it, he told himself, and fulsomely praised her purchase.

Isolde was no fool. "I wonder why you let me pick you up like this, Max," she murmured with a grin, and steered off the road into one of the new lay-bys. "Now, darling, I feel I must have all my wits about me for this. And if I don't like it, we're not so far out of the town, I can soon turn round and drive you back. What were you doing in that scruffy hole, anyway?"

"Thinking," he said, "and now I've thought, and I know just how I am going to put it to you. I want my freedom."

Isolde had always marvelled at the way Max had misread her. In the past, she had wondered why he hadn't bought her presents or taken the trouble to make love to her, when he wanted to ask her something. No, it was always this way, going at it bullheaded. Or, as Max himself might have said, man to man. Isolde was not flattered by the inference that her way of thinking was like a man. She said at once, "Certainly not. Quite apart from the way the Trusts are tied up, I wouldn't want it. Is that all?"

"No, it isn't. You don't want me. I've been out of your life for some years. You don't even use my name. I'd like *out*, Isolde."

"To go to some other woman? Go to her, my dear. I don't mind. But come back to me. That's how it is."

Max kept his temper and decided that a conversation in the car wasn't such a good idea. "I didn't say I wanted to marry again. I didn't say I wanted someone else. I just want to be finished with being tied to you. You should know that I was bound to chafe at the bonds of marriage without the blessings, Isolde."

"What an old-fashioned way of putting it, darling! Then if there is nobody else you want, then we must try and cook up some of the so-called blessings, as you put it," and she laughed.

And then she saw his face. For a fleeting moment his guard was down and she saw what she interpreted as dislike in his eyes. A slow angry flush crept up her cheeks. "No, I was wrong, wasn't I?" she breathed. The enormity of the thought that had struck her, almost choked her, as she remembered a bit of gossip her maid had imparted to her, fresh from the town. Her maid adored to give her titbits of gossip from one particular quarter. So the girl was right! "I should have guessed," Isolde hissed, "when you thought you could bargain with me about that wretched family at The Mill House, in return for your coming back to me. What a good thing I didn't agree!"

"What on earth are you talking about?" Max asked harshly.

"Gossip, my dear, the life and soul of this part of the world. I know just how many times you have been to The Mill House, and make very sure I have been informed the girl's a beauty. Quite unintelligent, I believe, but a beauty nevertheless, and our dear old Max always had an idea for beauty, no?"

"What on earth can you mean?" he asked blankly.

"I didn't believe it, when I heard you'd got into some accident so you had to actually stay overnight in that wretched place. I haven't been given the details yet, but I shall be, don't worry. And the answer's no, Max! No freedom, not now or ever!"

Max drove to The Mill House later that day. He had no reason to go there. He just couldn't keep away, and his visit wasn't very wise, since he was still so steamed up about that scene with Isolde. He pulled up at a point where he had discovered he could get a slanting view of The Mill House yet his car was out of sight. Deliberately he tried to relax, drink in the beauty, the silence of the country, the peace of it all, before he could get his thoughts together.

He had been a fool to expect Isolde to give him his freedom, of course. She was protected by those Trusts, drawn up by her three uncles to keep her married to a good sound man (as Max had once heard them describe him) and because they were good men, they hadn't even given a thought to the fact that their niece would take her pleasures where she liked, without benefit of clergy, and that in their way they had given her the perfect weapon to swiftly cut free from any man she tired of. Her marriage was for ever, the uncles had said, and had worked it out that way. Neither Isolde nor Max would be rich if they broke the Trusts and the marriage.

For perhaps the first time in all his life, Max regretted meeting someone: Carlotta. Having met her, his heart would ache for her till the end of time and he couldn't do a thing about it.

He wondered what she was doing at this moment and he decided that it would be more to the point if he stopped dreaming about her and went back to town to try and think of a way to stop Isolde smashing up the Buckland family by forcing them to leave The Mill House.

Steve stood under one of the trees that bordered the water below the great wheel and watched Max carefully turn his car, using the farm gate. What was that chap doing sitting there looking at the house, Steve asked himself angrily. Working out a way of making them go sooner than they could, he supposed. Steve was the only one of the family who didn't like Max, and that wasn't personal. It was simply because he had seen the way those two — Max and Carlotta — had looked at each other. He was only fourteen but he sensed the atmosphere. He would have felt the same about any other man who had exchanged such a look with Carlotta. He didn't feel the same way about Don Foxwell, who was miraculously not knocking nails in at this moment, but probably enjoying tea and Carly's newest batch of biscuits in The Mill House kitchen. Nor did he feel like it about Keith Anscombe, although he nursed the same conviction as the builder, that he would be Carly's husband one day: no rush, just one day. Each man was comfortably sure it would be himself, but to the children they were a comic couple, and the odds all seemed against Carly marrying either of them.

But Maxstead was another matter. He had come with confidence, at a time when they weren't expecting him. He was a stranger, a handsome charming stranger with a personality that was new to the young Bucklands. The aura of travel, working abroad, sat on him. They didn't know which public school he had been to, but could hazard guesses: Steve already had, in a way that had made his Uncle Fergus look sharply at him and realize the boy was growing up. And like Fergus, Steve was uncomfortably aware that it was not the threat of having The Mill House wrested from them that had upset them all in this strange way. No, it was the arrival in their lives of Max Jefferson that had done that.

He kicked a stone savagely into the water and went back into the house. The doctor had been up with Fergus and was now sitting with Carly in the small parlour. Nothing new in that. He often talked to Carly about the uncle's health. Steve was so incensed about Max that he didn't for the moment notice anything different in this meeting between the doctor and his sister Carlotta. He burst out, "I say, that chap's been sitting in his car up the lane, staring at the house," and he flushed with anger so that all his freckles started out singly.

It seemed a natural enough thing to him, to come into the house and burst out with whatever had annoyed him, in front of the doctor. They were so used to Guy Morrison around that he was practically family. But something was wrong. Carly went red, then white, and muttered something about, "Is he here now? I can't see him! No, wait, send him in . . . Where is he?" and the doctor glared at her and said, "Why, Carly?"

Jay called urgently to Steve. Puzzled, he went out and Jay slammed the parlour door. "Oh, you chump," she scolded Steve. "Fancy barging in there with those two, at a time like this! Haven't you *any* sense?"

Steve said, "Why shouldn't I go in? They weren't talking and the door was open. What's so special . . . "

"Well, it *was* special," Jay said, taking his arm and dragging him out the back into the yard. "I don't want to say it in front of Don, but we were hoping . . . oh, Steve, can't you *see*? Carly and Guy Morrison? It would be so nice, and Uncle Fergus wants it!"

Steve gaped at her, trying to take in what her words told her he must, but what his common sense wouldn't accept. The doctor and his sister were in two separate slots in his mind. He had never thought of them as a *pair*.

Neither had Carly, until that afternoon. It hadn't been any easy conversation.

Because of her own cooperation in the meeting, Guy Morrison had found himself at a loss for words. He had been going to say something nice and easy, on the lines of: "Carly, I don't think this will entirely surprise you, what I have to say. We've known each other a long time and I don't think you like me less than I like you," and from there it should have been (with the help of a few words from her, agreeing with him) fairly easy. But no sooner had they sat down, than she had turned to him and burst out: "It's Uncle Fergus, isn't it? He's worse, isn't he? Well, you don't ever ask to speak to me in this room, just ourselves, Guy. You usually follow me into the kitchen for tea and cake."

"But there are others in the kitchen today, Carly," he began.

"That's what I mean. So what did you want to say, so private? It *is* about Uncle Fergus, isn't it?"

He looked at her face, drawn and white, and her anxious eyes and he wanted to pull her into his arms and cuddle her and say easily, "He's no worse, my dear, but a man sometimes has something else private and personal to say to a girl," only Carly went on talking and he didn't get a chance.

"It's the worry of this place, you know, and all of us, and to be honest, Guy, I don't really mind if they make us sell this beastly house and go and live in a *normal* house."

It surprised him so much that he just sat and looked at her.

"Oh, I know you won't believe me, Guy, because we've always made such a big thing of how we liked this place, being different and all that. I suppose we were really kidding ourselves to make it more bearable. Okay, it's unusual . . . well, quaint, I suppose, would be the best word. But it isn't all that convenient. Too many stairs. No fun trying to get bath-water hot, and when people say we don't have to worry about industrial trouble over gas, coal, electricity, things like that, because we're floating in wood for the fires, I feel like saying, just try lighting a fire with damp wood after a storm or the mill-stream flooding."

"Carly, my dear, I had no idea you felt like that!" Guy said. "I had the impression when that chap came the other night to tell you all that Lady Powley wanted to sell the land . . ."

Carly turned on him quite unexpectedly. "Why do you refer to Max Jefferson as 'that chap'? He's got a name, you know. You sound as if you don't like him. What's he done to upset you?"

Guy wasn't prepared for it. He said, without thinking, "Well, I could say several things, though he might not have even noticed them. That's his trouble, he goes through life confidently expecting everyone to applaud him. He can do no wrong, and he's so sure of women thinking so. You've only known him a few hours, Carly, and you're acting like the rest. Well, at least *I'm* not years older than you are, and I *am* a bachelor!"

She ignored the remark about how old Max was and concentrated on the other point. "You mean . . . he's not a bachelor? He's been married?"

And it was at that quite unfortunate point that Steve hurtled in to angrily say that Max was sitting in his car outside.

All Carly wanted to do was to see him, ask him if it were true, what the doctor had said. And then all at once she didn't want to know. Her thoughts jostled round in her head. It wasn't true! Max would have told her if he'd been married, and anyway, what did it matter if he were a widower, her bewildered thoughts raced? Come to think of it, he certainly had an easier manner than the doctor, the sort of manner a man had when he had once been married. It was a reflex action to tell Steve to fetch Max in. But Jay had, as usual, turned the situation, ruined everything. Poor Jay, so beautiful, so lovable, and such a clot, always putting her foot in it. To drag Steve away like that, and shut the door, had something of the Victorian melodrama about it, but at the same time it alerted Carly as nothing else could have done, as to what the doctor had brought her in this room to talk about, so privately. She flushed furiously and her embarrassment communicated itself to him. "Guy, I don't want to talk any more. Not today. I've got cakes in the oven, anyway, and there's the meal."

The doctor grasped the tail end of his chance and it wasn't the right thing to do. "I would make you a good husband, Carlotta."

If he had said he loved her, anything, anything at all, but that flat statement somehow set her against him. "Please, please, dear Guy, don't say any more. I can't . . . oh, it simply isn't on. Can't you see I'm dotty about someone else?" And then she dashed her hand to her mouth, furious that she'd said so much, and fled from the room.

There wasn't anywhere really private in The Mill House. She shared a room with Jay and the kitchen always had people in it or coming and going. Uncle Fergus was not the refuge today, as apparently he had heard about Guy's intentions and thoroughly approved of them. Carly fled out of the back door, through the kitchen garden, down along the edge of the stream and on to the small stone bridge over the road that Max's car had recently come down. Under the bridge was a dry patch and dense bushes. Carly, in a faded green cotton dress, was almost hidden there. Almost but not quite. Max had come back. Irritably, he hadn't been able to keep away and had invented something to say to Carly, if she should come out. But when he saw her, she was flying, blind to her whereabouts, through the garden to the bridge. He pulled up beyond it, in the opening where Steve had seen him. He left the car there and walked quietly back to where Carly was crouched, silently crying.

Fergus had been upset over that silent grief of hers; Max was completely overset. Without thinking what he was doing, he quietly pulled her into his arms and she clung to him. It was as simple as that. Two people without the need for explanation, apology, anything; two people drawn to each other without the need to even think of words.

The big dog found them and stood, pulled up short, puzzled, and turned to see how young Holly took it. Holly, at six, wasn't easily put out of her stride, but slithering down the side of the stone bridge to see what the dog had found to interest him, she was certainly struck. Max's face was turned to her, his eyes closed. He could only think of Isolde refusing to give him his freedom, and here was Carly breaking her heart and he had no right to comfort her.

Holly put her fingers to her lips and crept away, the big dog doing a fair parody of her soft-padding footsteps. Holly only knew one source of comfort: the uncle. She found him looking worried. She said, without preamble, "Uncle Fergus, our Carly's crying on that nice Max's shoulder, down by the bridge, and that nice Max is crying too, and — " She frowned, as her uncle put his hand over his eyes in despair. This was the last thing he had wanted to hear. "And now you're crying, Uncle Fergus. Should I cry?"

"No, child. It's just disappointment. You know how you felt when you'd been promised that trip into Fenborough and it rained all day and you couldn't go? Well, that's just how I feel."

"You're not really well enough to go to Fenborough, though," the literal Holly commented, and he agreed. "And that's not making me feel any happier, love," he commented, pulling her on to his knees. "Where are all the others?"

"Steve's been ticked off by Jay for going in the parlour to talk to Carly and the doctor, only Carly didn't look as if she wanted to talk to him. What's the matter with everyone today, Uncle Fergus?"

"Well, let's say . . . Holly, would you mind if we had to leave this house?"

he asked her, not only sidetracking her but because he really wanted to know.

"I don't know. I don't suppose I'd mind if we went to a nice house near the shops. I'd like to be near shops and buses and the Pictures.

"What about the others? How do they feel?"

"Why don't you ask them, Uncle Fergus?"

"Well, I daresay I will, but you're a wise little person and I rather like having your version, you know."

That thrilled Holly. "Oh, well, let's see," she said, ticking them off on her fat little fingers. "Jay would like to be near the town because she hates going in on her bike in the winter. Amy's the same. She wants to go to the vet's on Saturdays and the holidays *as well*, and that's going to be awkward, right out here."

Fergus nodded. "And Steve wants Horticultural College so it won't matter for him," he murmured and, seeing the child's guilty look, he gave her a hug and said, "Don't tell him I guessed, but he keeps looking in the newspapers just around now, when they put in the names and addresses of schools around. Let's keep it a secret. What about Carlotta?" he asked, in an off-hand voice that fooled the child.

"I think she hates The Mill House because there's so much hard work to do," Holly said frankly. "Would we sell it or have to give it to that horrible old Lady Powley?"

"We can sell the house, love, because it belongs to us."

"But she wants to knock it down!"

"It's called 'development' and a lot of houses get knocked down if they've got a lot of land round them without anything built on them."

"Why can't she just ask the men to build round us?"

Fergus frowned and growled, "Well, *I* for one wouldn't like to have a lot of new buildings all around us. Much better to go into a town and have all the other things we wanted, like the

127

Pictures and ice-cream." But his heart was heavy. They'd all been keeping it a secret that they didn't like living here. He hadn't got their confidence, just when he thought he had.

7

ISOLDE listened with half an ear to her new solicitor. She didn't like him. He had seemed a smart new asset at first. Acquiring him had been a matter of breaking with tradition, breaking with her old uncle's lawyers who reeked of the establishment, law and order. Her new solicitor was somehow bending with the times, smiling sardonically at all that was responsible, traditional, conventional. Now he was just a bore and she wanted to be rid of him, and he was no help whatever to her. The gist of his long conversation with her now was to the effect that she couldn't stop Max getting his freedom if he wanted to break the Trusts and finish up very hard up. "He might want to marry big money, and not care. Handsome chap, big, the brutal type."

That was a wild exaggeration, she thought bitterly. She wouldn't have minded so much, she found herself thinking angrily, if Max *had* been the brutal type. He was so big and handsome, but so gentle in his love-making. If he had hurt her, things might have been different. She found it difficult to breathe, now, as she thought of it.

"He's not going to get his freedom," she muttered. "Besides, I don't believe he's got any heiress lined up. He still needs the money.

"And then again," her solicitor went on, ignoring that, "there's the question of a scandal. You really can't afford that, you know, as things are."

"Tell me something I don't know," she snapped, remembering Uncle Joseph's fanatical uprightness, and demanding the same quality in all his young relatives. "Can't you think of *something*?"

"Yes, you could make a great show of being kind to The Mill House people and letting them off the hook, and

I think he would shut up then. He rather likes that lot, you know. Can't think why."

"Tell me about them," she asked suddenly. "Don't tell me I ought to know — why should I?"

He looked uncomfortable. "Not much good at describing things," he muttered.

"How many of them are there living there? Nobody seems willing to let me know the awful truth," she said angrily.

"Oh, several," he said vaguely. "I'm not sure. There's the old man, the uncle, you know. He seems to be in charge. There always seem to be young children drifting all over the place. You're on sticky ground there, you know. Everyone's sympathy goes to a family of young children when their roof is taken away from them."

"Oh, hell, Winters, what a lot of rot you talk!" she stormed. "Who cares? How many?"

"Well, there is the ravishing beauty," he added uncomfortably, suddenly realising that that was what Isolde wanted to hear. It would be important to her to know whether there was anyone there who could interest her husband, since she was plainly puzzled as to why he should take up the cause of a family hitherto unknown to him.

"Ah-h, so that is the crunch we are coming to," she said, her eyes glittering with anger. "So now we know why Master Max goes over there so much."

"Oh, no, I don't really think — " the unhappy solicitor (newly appointed here and torn between pleasing Isolde and not infuriating the large and powerful Max Jefferson, who had the trick of looking at Winters as if he were a horrid little insect creeping out from under a stone) tried to keep nicely in the middle so as not to offend anyone.

Isolde misunderstood. "You're shielding Max. Well, you needn't bother. I know my husband very well. He can have his beauty, but he won't have his freedom to marry her, and no, I will not reconsider. Even if I didn't want the rotten project, I would push ahead, so as to get those people out.

"But the house is theirs. You'll have to give them the market price for it — ," he pointed out, but that made her laugh.

"What market price? The place is ramshackle! All right, all right, we'll give them a price, and they can go into a nasty little house in a nasty little street, and I'll tear down the wretched Mill. I'm tired of hearing about it."

"Take your time. Think about it and wonder if it's worth it," Winters urged. The village might be glad to hear of the project, but he was quite sure that any other project would make them happy if it was going to provide work, and after the manner of people in a place like Cheltonwood, they would remember at an uncomfortable time that Lady Powley also turned out the Buckland family. Nobody who had anything to do with that project would be popular. That was the way of people.

He led the conversation into the safer

waters of discussing another deal she had in mind, and hoped that The Mill House would be allowed to drift on. He didn't personally know the Bucklands, but he did know that the district liked them and that the children were also beautiful and clever. And he purposely hadn't mentioned Carlotta, because he remembered in time that the doctor was interested in her, and that the doctor's uncle was a client of his and also on the local Council. He sighed. He had been so keen to get this work for Lady Powley but now he wasn't so sure he'd done the right thing. People had a trick of looking at him as if they were comparing his slight size with the hefty handsome Maxstead, and he softly cursed the husband of Lady Powley for coming back from wherever he'd been working abroad and stirring all this up. After all the chap had done with raising hell over getting his freedom all this time: what did he want to stir things up now for? And was he really keen on one of those girls at The Mill House?

Rumours were flying around. Nothing new in a district like this, but they sometimes were partly true . . .

Max was thinking of Lady Powley as he sat there holding Carly to him. Neither of them was aware that the dog and young Holly had been so near, nor that Steve had seen them. They were conscious only of each other.

Carly had finished crying. She looked tired and spent, and then became aware of who she was with; aware of the comfort of leaning against Max's shoulder. She looked sharply around her and pushed away from him but he held her firmly, partly as a reflex action, and partly because there wasn't a lot of room for moving, if they didn't want to slither down into the stream. "What are you doing here?" she asked hoarsely.

"I came back, to ask you something. I saw you run down here. What were you crying for?" His choice of words didn't sound sharp, he spoke them so softly, and Carly could see no way

135

round them. She must answer him. Then anger flared in her.

"Guy Morrison asked me to marry him. Then he said things about you and I got wild and . . . I don't suppose he'll speak to me again. But that's not the point. It's what he said. Is it true?"

It wasn't like Carly to be incoherent. What she meant was, 'he said that at least he was a bachelor and you weren't, and he wasn't years older than me'. She would have actually said those words if she'd thought it mattered, but she didn't, and Max thought she'd discovered he was Lady Powley's husband, and so there wasn't any point in making things worse. He said quietly, "I'm sorry, Carly. I did try to tell you, once or twice, but somehow we got interrupted. I'd better go abroad again, though, I don't know how I'm going to manage to leave you."

"Why would you go abroad again?" Her head was thudding from too much crying and she couldn't even focus straight, let alone sort out her thinking.

"Because . . . I seem to have fallen in love with you, and I don't think I ever loved anyone else like it in my whole life and it's . . . too much of a mess all round. Heaven knows what your uncle will say if he gets to hear of it."

She only heard the first part of all that and her face slid into a smile of such dazzling warmth that he couldn't say anything else. "Well, I don't really mind," she said thickly, wondering why Uncle Fergus should mind that Max was a widower and some years older than she was. Then she recalled that Uncle Fergus had shown some dislike for Max from the start. "I'll tell him I love you, too, and it'll be all right," she said, rather thickly, as if she were a little drunk, and she leaned against him, blindly waiting for him to kiss her.

"Carly, for heaven's sake!" Max exploded, putting her from him, then as her feet began to slither downwards, he caught her to him again and held her. "Carlotta Buckland, have a bit of sense!" he growled, giving her a shake.

"I may be said to be all sorts of . . . well, I don't suppose anyone's got a good word to say for me, the way people are . . . but I believe I have some principles left!"

"So long as you don't pretend to be rich, like you did last time, I don't mind what you do," she murmured. To Carly, that really was an important thing.

"What have you got against me having a great deal of money?" he asked in the sort of frustrated voice that always put her back up.

She leaned back, frowning. "There you go again!" she exploded. "If there's one kind of man I can't stand, it's the sort who boasts about how he made money and then you find out it's all a tall story and he hasn't got a bean. Max, I don't care that you're hard up. So are we! Only don't pretend, darling. I could never trust you again, don't you see? People must be honest, with me."

She stared into his eyes and he couldn't help himself. He shook his head a little and then succumbed to her lovely mouth, upturned to his and inviting him in a way that was almost innocent. He kissed her, holding the back of her head in one hand, and he didn't seem to be able to stop.

Yet it was Max himself, and not Carly, who finally broke away, muttering, "I must be mad. Come on, girl, let's get you back to the house," and he took her hand and pulled her up the bank.

"Come and see Uncle Fergus and let's tell him," she said, dreamily.

"I don't think your Uncle Fergus's condition will be improved by being told how we feel about each other, my dear," he said tautly, bringing Carly down to earth with a bump at the very tone of his voice. "In fact, I think he'll be a lot better in health and spirits if we don't let him know."

Fergus had gone to bed. He hadn't been feeling well again. Jay had got some sort of scratch supper for them all. Jay was sincere, she loved them all, she adored to help Carly if she could, but the curious thing was, she never managed to make a decent meal. If she and Carly had both set out to use the same things out of the store cupboard, Carly would have turned out a princely repast, but Jay's effort would be just tins opened and dumped on the plates. She said now, "It's only tinned steak, Carly, and it burnt a bit, and I didn't stop to do chips. Is that all right?" and she smiled, her heartbreakingly beautiful smile. She really was a beautiful young woman, Max thought. It made him uneasy for some reason. He didn't want Isolde to know how beautiful Jay was, yet how Isolde would ever be concerned with any member of the family at The Mill House, he couldn't think, at that moment.

"Is your pal staying to supper?" Jay asked naturally, but she avoided looking at them. Jay had expected the doctor to stay and announce that he and Carly were to be married. No point in thinking that any longer, she told herself, after taking a look at the faces of Carly and that Max Jefferson!

Max said hastily, "No, thanks, I just wanted to see Carly safely indoors. I think she's got a rotten head or something. Hope you'll be more fit tomorrow, lass," he said, with a nice casual tone, and, waving goodnight to them all, he slipped away. Carly's disappointment was embarrassing to the rest of them.

Little Holly said, "What's everyone looking like that for? Don't we have to like that nice Max any more?"

They all spoke at once and Carly quietly sat down to table, but got up again to make the coffee, which Jay had forgotten.

Jay thought, 'I must be careful not to look like that when Richard comes over next time', and worried about what she should say to Steve, when he tackled her — as he surely would — about the way she had hustled him out of the parlour.

Steve was still incensed about it. He didn't begin to understand. He had liked Max at first, then when he saw how he was obviously interested in his sister Carly, he had felt all different; protective towards Carlotta, hostile towards Max. Then it seemed that the doctor was to marry Carly, and now it seemed as if things had swung away again, and Carly herself was interested in Max. Steve was at the age when he liked things to be said, plain and in the open. He felt itchy and uncomfortable if he knew someone was pretending, keeping some information dark, as now. He said suddenly, "I don't like that Max!"

Carlotta looked thoughtfully at him. She had got herself under control again and knew she wouldn't shake or flush or feel high as she had when she had come in from the bridge with Max. Something wasn't quite right about the things he had said, and the thought of it had rather toned down her sudden excitement. Now she said to Steve, "But you don't know him well enough to like him, or not, love."

"Yes, I do! People are talking about

him in the village."

"There's always gossip in Cheltonwood. You know that, Steve."

Jay was glaring at him. Steve felt lost when both his sisters appeared to be hiding something. He pushed his plate away. "I can't eat that. I don't know what you do with the food, Jay. Anyway, I don't know what you do to everything! You make a mess of everything you touch — except your music, of course!"

Jay had whitened, but looked happier at his last few words, but now Carly was upset. "Steve, what can you mean, talking to Jay like that?"

"Well," the boy exploded, "she threw me out of the parlour because it was supposed to be the doctor asking you to marry him and now you come in all soppy about that Max and he can't marry you! I think you two are mad!"

Jay got to her feet and screamed, "Steve, *shut up*!" at the same time as Carly got to her feet and begged Steve to make clear what he had meant. The boy shrugged.

"Hark at you both now! One of you wants me to talk, and the other doesn't. I think you're a soppy couple. I'm quite sure the doctor didn't want to marry anyone, and that Max can't marry anyone — he's married already. Well," he said, backing away from the angry Jay, "if you didn't know he was that ole Lady Powley's husband, where've you been all this time? Everyone knows it!"

Jay's music lesson was the next day and she had never felt less like playing the piano, but it had to be done. She worked all her waking hours to get these piano lessons and she wasn't going to let a family storm stop her if she could help it. Every pound counted, every hour counted, towards that mythical time when somehow, somehow, she would go to Paris to study.

Anyway, it would be wonderful to get away from the rest of them. It had been awful last night. She hoped she'd never see Carlotta look like that again. It seemed as if, in those few minutes when Steve had hurled his bombshell, their elder sister had become a mature, heartbroken woman. Yet how, why? As Steve had said, was it possible that nobody had told Carly?

It was that job that she had just given up, Jay supposed. When Carly had come home at week-ends, there had been too much for her to do to catch up on the housework, the washing and sewing, and the planning for someone else to carry on all week, for her to pay much attention to what was being said about people outside The Mill House. Perhaps, come to think of it, they hadn't said anything much about Lady Powley. It was one of those subjects one absorbed, from bits of odd conversation over a period of time, and didn't think it worth acquainting anyone else with. Anyway, Carly hadn't known, and now she did.

What a mess it all was! Holly had

stared, her eyes big with awe, as the voices of her brother and sisters lashed back and forth, and then Uncle Fergus had come down and wanted to know what it was about, and he had looked dreadful. And now he was in bed, sick.

It was her own fault, Jay told herself wretchedly, for trying to pair off Carly with the doctor, yet she had thought Uncle Fergus had wanted that too. It would have been such a neat way out. And now, staring them in the face, was this business of their having to leave The Mill House, and quite plainly poor old Uncle Fergus didn't want to go, and didn't think the rest of them did either, and how on earth could they tell him that they all wanted to leave the rotten place? Holly didn't, of course. At least, the child had no thoughts either way, as far as she knew.

The music lesson didn't go well. Her teacher sat back and said, "We shall have to scrub today's lesson, won't we? What went wrong, Jewel?" Nothing on earth would make him call her Jay, like the rest of the family. A name was a name and, when she had begun her lessons, he had told her severely to get used to the one that would be on the posters outside concert halls, if she made it.

"Do you know Lady Powley?" she asked, for no good reason. The name was on her mind and she had to talk to someone, though she didn't suppose her teacher would know the woman.

He did, as it happened. "What about her?"

"What's she like?"

"Why do you want to know, Jewel?"

"Well, actually it's a bit personal. A family thing. You know she's our ground landlord, of course."

"It's this thing about you all having to leave The Mill House? My dear girl, everybody knows about that. Believe me, we're all on your side, but I believe there's nothing that can be done. The weight of money, you know."

Jay's face crumpled. Childishly she put her hands up to her cheeks and closed her eyes tightly, unaware of her teacher's pain-filled face. To Jay, nobody had any problems or hurts or heartaches except the Buckland family, so she would not have understood if she could have glanced at poor Edward Yates's face just then. He was a man who was difficult to put in any age group. Thin, bespectacled, his brown hair so grizzled with oncoming grey that it was not easy to decide what colour it was. He wore it neither long nor short, but an unhappy in-between which didn't matter at all because nobody really looked at him. He was the bespectacled, gowned organist, choir-master and teacher of local music students. Like the proverbial postman, it was what he wore and how he walked, always clutching music, which people noticed.

So it was that Jay didn't look at him but used him as an empty vacuum to fill with her own misery. Without mentioning names and blandly forgetting the possibility that even this remote personage would know who she was talking about she tumbled out what was bothering her.

"There's not one of us who cares if we stay at The Mill House except our uncle and that's because he's old-fashioned and ill and terribly hard up."

Edward Yates winced. How uncaring the young were, in the words they used to paint a picture! He knew Fergus Buckland and liked him.

"And I thought," Jay continued, "I was being very clever in pairing off one of my sisters to a doctor, to get free treatment for our uncle and take one of us off his hands, and it messed everything up because I didn't know she'd fallen for someone else, someone who isn't free and our uncle doesn't know and she's only just found out because we couldn't keep our mouths shut. Oh, and I *must* make a go of my music so I can become a great pianist and rescue them all before they get too hard up to help, and I'm scared of what Lady Powley can do because everyone says she's such a blight and she's got enough money to pay people to do her dirty work — "

Edward Yates leapt to sudden life. This must stop before it became really dangerous. It was not his policy to touch any student, so he did for him what was the next best thing. Jewel's lovely mouth must be closed so he lifted one of her own hands and pressed it to her full red lips, much to her surprise. Her eyes snapped open and met his angry ones. "Jewel, this must not go on!" he said firmly. "All right, you had to unload on someone. Lucky for you that it was me, because I am well known for being able to keep a tightly closed mouth. Also you are lucky to be here with me, in one of the music-rooms in the church hall where we are not likely to be overheard. But promise me, promise me you will not say any of this aloud to anyone, any more! Promise!"

"But I didn't mention names," Jay pouted.

"Do you think that amounts to anything, in a place like this?" he asked wryly. "Now, listen to me. You are unhappy, and that is bad for your music. You must forget about the domestic troubles. My dear child, they have a habit of righting themselves, without anyone else's help. Perhaps because of the absence of outside help! So leave them alone. I'm sure your sister won't thank you for interfering!"

Jay remembered Carlotta's face, so calm, so expressionless, but those usually quiet eyes of hers were smouldering pools of anger. Never had Jay seen her sister look like that before. And not a word about it was said! Even Steve caught on that he had upset Carly very seriously; they hadn't seen him since, except for snatched mealtimes!

"But how can everything be put right?" she asked miserably.

"Well, consider your own life. Tell me what you think you will do about it — in every way?

"Well, I won't stay at home any longer than I have to," Jay said roundly. "Everyone knows I'm a rotten cook and

I'm a blunderbuss — I like to help people but somehow my help only adds to the confusion."

Edward Yates's lips twitched. Ten years older than Jay, and looking a good ten years older than that, he was not a person Jay would consider capable of understanding, or finding such a thing funny, but he did. Tenderly funny. He said, "Well, we can't all be comfortable capable people who can swoop on chaos and instantly put all to rights."

Jay's eyes opened wide. "But that's what my sister's like! How did you *know*?"

"Well, I didn't know. I was just thinking of the sort of person you seem to want to be like. That sort of person is born, not made. You were born to love music and — " he would have liked to say, 'and be beautiful' but that would not have done at all. He said instead, " — and you should be thankful that that is the one thing you can do, provided you are not in a fret of worry over things that are really other people's concern."

"Oh, but it isn't — the only thing I'm good at, I mean. I'm really good at dressmaking. That's how I get money for my lessons," she said, in a burst of confidence, and then was wretched because she was quite sure Carly would be furious if she knew that Jay had said that. Okay, some women in the town knew, but it was a thing they seemed to keep to themselves, and not discuss with the men. Jay, who blurted everything out, had never understood the niceties of such things. If you weren't ashamed of doing a thing, why not talk about it?

"Well, then, you have less to worry about than I at first thought, for that surely is a job that will never stop. A dressmaker is always required. Isn't that so?"

Vastly comforted, Jay looked a little closer at him and was surprised to find that he wasn't the old man she had always thought of him as. Probably forty or fifty, she thought comfortably, and proceeded to tell him other things she should have kept to herself. "Do you know Lady Powley's husband? That nice Max? Oh, there was frightful trouble over him!"

Edward Yates sighed. "I have as much curiosity as the next person and I would dearly like to know just what the trouble was, but I won't ask you. You are not to say, Jewel. I'm quite sure it's far too personal to talk to a stranger about — "

"But that's the odd thing about it. Suddenly you're not a stranger but a friend. A good friend!" she said, wonderingly, and was bothered because he went a bright pink, then whitened. "Are you all right?" she asked, in a scared voice.

"No, I am not! I'm wondering how I can impress on you what these words mean: 'if it doesn't concern *you*, don't talk about it!' Got it?"

"Yes, but it does concern me! It was all my fault. That's just it! I meddled. I'm always meddling. At least, I think

I'm helping at the time and it's only afterwards, when I see the result, that I realise it was meddling all the time. What shall I do?"

"Has Max Jefferson told you you have been meddling?" he asked carefully.

"Oh, you know him! The thing is, *we* all found out pretty quickly that he was Lady Powley's husband only somehow Carly *didn't* know, and that's the awful part about it. And no, he wouldn't say such a thing to me, because he's a real gentleman."

Edward Yates thought about Max. He had played the organ for Max's wedding and had thought at the time that *there* was a man who was not head over heels in love with his bride, but a man who was determined to do the proper thing from start to finish. Rumour had it that he was pleasing an elderly relative of his and the three powerful wealthy uncles of Lady Powley. He had never been clear in those days why Max had been chosen to marry Isolde. He had no money at all. He was the younger son of an earl but of course — as the elder son had married and got an heir — never had a hope in the world of a title, and Lady Powley had a title from her first husband, Sir Henry, who had got a knighthood in politics and had been thirty years her senior and only lived a year after their marriage. But he had heard a bit of gossip from the woman secretary of one of the uncles, that in their opinion Isolde was at last getting 'a *man*' for her husband, and all three of the uncles were vastly pleased. He could see their point. In his opinion Lady Isolde had been a pain in the neck ever since she was a child. A spoilt brat, a not particularly nice brat with or without the spoiling. Without thinking, Edward murmured, "Yes, you could say that about him with complete truth."

"Oh, you know him then!" Jay sounded delighted. Then, her face clouding, she said, "But why is he being friends with our Carly, when he's a married man. He must know . . . our family wouldn't like that."

"I think you can trust him completely," Edward Yates said.

"Then you must know him very well, to say that! That's a relief!"

"I wouldn't say I know him well," he protested, then, drawing a deep breath, he said, "Well, perhaps I do, though he may not know it. Three things about him I remember well, which I think qualify for my having the warmest admiration for him as a man." He wondered if he were right in gossiping, but if it would help Jay Buckland, why not? "I was driving along Cornhill Lane one foggy night in winter," he said, his mind going back over the past. "This was long before Max Jefferson went abroad. It was a beast of a night. I was pushing slowly along. You know how narrow it is, with a deep dyke on the other side of the hedge. Then I saw lights through the fog and as I stopped my car I heard a lot of shouting. There was a big black car pulled up." He still wondered if he were doing the right thing in recounting this story. "Well, to cut a long story short, it was poor little Farmer Mathieson's new cow stuck in the dyke. He's not a big man, and his sons were away, and only one man helping him. Then I saw that Max Jefferson was in it up to the neck, and without him they'd never had got the animal out. He was in evening dress, on his way to a party. He could have driven on, got help for the farmer in the town, though it might have been too late. But no, he just went into the thick of it himself. He's a powerful chap and . . . well, that's one incident."

Jay shivered delicately. Frankly farming and animals bored her stiff but she couldn't help remarking, "My sister Amy would be thrilled with that story. She's crazy over animals. She wants to be a vet. She won't, though. We'd never be able to afford the training."

"Well, the second occasion I remember was the same winter. Old Vic Smithson had got a job every year at Fellows Store in Fenborough as Father Christmas.

You know the sort of thing. Poor old boy relied on it, because the store was good to him and besides his wages they gave him a small hamper to take home. That year he had trouble at home. One of his daughters had been ill in hospital and they diagnosed a lung thing she'd never get over. The old boy got drunk to drown his sorrows and couldn't be Father Christmas. Well, what store would have a drunken chap in that job? He hung about and watched the substitute Santa Claus do a marvellous job, and wondered why a young chap should be given it. Yes, you got it! Max Jefferson had heard about it, and took on the job so they should keep it open for old Smithson next year."

"Why didn't he just give him money?" the practical Jay asked, not considering that a very good story.

"The store didn't recognise Max, and anyway, Max hadn't got a bean. He married Isolde for her money, people will tell you. All I know is, he was absolutely without funds and she kept him. And don't you breathe a word about all this, young lady. Have I your promise?"

"He must like children. I wouldn't be Santa, if I were a man. A week or two of pure agony, from what I've seen of it," Jay said, and hastily gave the required promise. "What's the third story?"

Edward baulked at telling it. One thing to say that Max had stopped a run-away horse by leaping at it and hanging on to the bridle and being dragged along. She would want to know why the clever fellow hadn't leapt up on the saddle. How could Edward tell her Isolde was riding it, and lashed at him with her crop until he let go? The horse was quiet by then. If Edward told Jay all that, he would have to admit how he came to see the incident. At that particular hunt meeting, the farmers and anyone who liked to ride a hack could go along. Edward liked riding, though he didn't go to the head of the hunt nor be in at the kill. He just liked the cross-country ride, and the sight of the local Hunt in their hunting pink, their fine mounts, their rules, the different notes on the horn and the chance of seeing the fox when no-one else did, all this appealed to him. He had been a straggler when the incident had happened. He had kept out of sight and wasn't surprised to hear that Max had gone abroad after that. That must have been in the thick of their rows that people had long since stopped talking about. But Jay was adamant, so he said briefly, "He stopped a runaway horse, riding to hounds. He's a very powerful chap, you know, and good at almost everything."

He couldn't know how utterly dismayed Jay felt. Even, in her consideration, if Max had been free, he must only have been briefly infatuated with her sister, for what had Carly in common with him? She didn't ride, let alone join the Hunt — nor did she do any of the things his set did. She was as Edward Yates had described her: a lovely, competent, comforting person. Their own Carly, and Jay was suddenly aware, although she hadn't much insight, that their own Carly was going to be, before their very eyes, crushed and heartbroken.

8

THERE was a storm on, when Fergus was again taken ill. Carly couldn't decide whether it was the sudden change in the weather, or the fact that he had been worrying about her, that had brought on this new attack. And the doctor couldn't be found. Some of the telephone lines were down and their own means of transport — the old bike — was out of the question. Carly did her best. She was no mean home nurse, but this was different. His colour was different.

It was evening and the whole family was at home, so that was one less thing to worry about. Carly often worried about Jay getting to The Mill House from the town in bad weather. The school bus transported the young ones.

Carly decided to try the telephone lines again, but even as she watched the lightning struck a tree which brought down the nearby telephone line and that meant that they themselves were cut off.

Jay burst in, forgetting to be quiet. Carly turned on her, finger to lips, but Uncle Fergus's eyes opened.

"Don't keep me out of what's going on," he said in a spent voice. "I'm not all that bad. What's wrong?"

Jay couldn't say. She stared at them both in a distracted way, then went out of the room and stood at the window, her shoulders shaking. A car softly started up and left the gate.

Carly slipped out. "Who was that in the car?" she demanded.

"Richard," Jay choked, and stemmed her tears with an effort.

"Did you tell him about Uncle Fergus? Well, why not? He could have found the doctor for us!"

Jay looked at Carly as if her sister had gone mad. "You don't stop having a row with your boyfriend to say, Oh, and on the way into town, look for the doctor for my uncle, or do you? Have a bit of sense, Carly!"

"You've had a row with Richard? Why?"

Jay shut her lips in a thin tight line. "Never mind. I was a fool to think he was different. Anyway, I should have made a push to find out more about him. Oh, never mind! Leave me alone!"

Another crash of thunder came and a fir-tree fell with a splash across the stream. Carly stared out of the window at it, her heart sinking to her boots. That would make a dam more effective than the local badger could and they would be flooded in no time.

Oh, this horrible house! Why, *why* did Uncle Fergus want to stay here? She slipped into the other bedrooms. Holly had been despatched to bed early and had hidden under the covers, but had somehow forgotten the storm and fallen asleep. Carly looked at the child's hot little face, so appealing in sleep, and she pushed the damp curls back.

Amy looked in and, seeing her sister was asleep, nodded and tiptoed out.

Carly caught her up on the landing. "Look, love, someone's got to go and find a telephone that's working."

"Steve? He's covering his plants," Amy said, pulling a face.

"No, it's got to be me. I can't have any of the rest of you out in this storm. Now look, pet, you're a sensible girl. Help Jay get supper for the rest of you, will you? It's only sausages, and I've taught you how to cook them without burning them. Now you try and show me what you can do."

Amy was being persuaded because it was Carly asking her. "I'll be as quick as I can, Amy, pet."

"Are you going to take the bike?" Should she tell Carly something was wrong with it? Steve was hoping he could somehow repair it before Carly knew.

"No, I'll wrap up and cross the fields to the telephone box at the crossroads. If that isn't working, I'll call in at

Matthieson's farm and see if one of the boys will drive me into town in one of their trucks. Now you mind me what I say — don't let Jay shout and carry on. Be quite calm and pleasant. Jay has had a row with Richard, and let him go without asking him to help."

Amy flushed and looked away. Carly caught her shoulder.

"What's the matter? You know what the row was about!"

"Carly, you're hurting my shoulder," the child protested. "I'll tell you. I heard. We all did. They were yelling so. His name isn't Richard at all — well, if it is, it's his second name. The thing is, he's only that ole Tim Roberts. The one we keep hearing about but who meets Uncle Fergus in Trowstock. You know, the agent for Lady Powley."

"But, why, why?" Carly was as bewildered as no doubt Jay was. "Why couldn't he say who he was at the first?"

"He told Jay he was sure she wouldn't want to be friends with him if she knew he worked for Lady Powley. He isn't going to work for her for ever. He wanted to be friends with Jay with nothing against him. Don't you think that's a funny thing to say?"

Carly was thinking, 'No, the funny thing is that Max Jefferson said he knew Tim Roberts well, and he was all right, so what sort of lies was Max Jefferson telling about his precious friend?' but all she said to the child was, "Jay will be upset, so be kind to her. Will you, love?"

"I'd rather be kind to you, Carly. Jay's so horrible if she feels a fool about something."

"Try, love. I must go and find the doctor for uncle."

She put on her old heavies: thigh-boots, the shiny raincoat and hood that was really waterproof and the great black umbrella. But in the event, she found the umbrella was no use — the wind blew it inside out — and her feet stuck in mud and her foot came out of one boot, leaving it behind. By the time she got to the crossroads, there was no need to try the telephone. Someone had put an Out of Order sign in to save the time and trouble of others. But there was a car creeping along the road, one that she recognised.

Max put his head out. "Good heavens, girl, you're drenched. Get in, do! I was going to try and reach The Mill House when I heard the lines were all down."

She hesitated, but you couldn't argue with Max. She had always known that. He opened the back door, took her wrist and yanked her in. "Get those wet things off, and tell me what you're doing alone, in a storm like this."

"Looking for the doctor. Uncle's been taken ill again."

He saw her white face and unforgiving eyes in the mirror, but merely nodded, turned the car in a side lane, with difficulty, since it was so rutted and sticky with churned-up mud, and drove towards Fenborough.

Carly said, "Why — " but he cut

across. "Your uncle's ill. You want a doctor. Your man is tied up at the Grey's farm and he'll be there all night. Want your uncle to die?" It was rough treatment, but it silenced Carly. "You'd better have our man," Max added. "He's competent. He'll come if I say so."

There was about ten minutes left to them to talk, if they were going to, Max thought. He would be bringing back Lady Powley's doctor and there would be no private talking after that! So he said, "What is it, Carly? Why are you angry with me? What did I say?"

"Why didn't you tell me you were Lady Powley's husband, from the start?"

He was so astonished, she felt the car twitch sideways as he lost the steering for a second. Then he said, "But I thought you did know! You said — "

She thought back over what had been said. "I got it into my head that you had been married before and were a widower. Everyone said things which

170

suggested that. It was Steve who said it outright. I would have appreciated it if you, yourself, had told me first."

"I can't see how you didn't know, Carlotta. But of course, it explains a lot of things. Now all I want to do is to help your uncle, because of the family friendship. You remember I told you." It seemed to him the safest line to take and he was right. After a second, Carly eased out and muttered, "It's . . . good of you to trouble. I'm grateful."

And that was all they said. Partly because the going was so rough and he had to concentrate on the driving; partly because he was afraid of further antagonising her. But what a way for two people to travel, he thought, in the close confines of a car on a night like this, when both of them were in love! Well, she had said she loved him and she wouldn't lie. And he loved her . . . It should have been easy for him to say, 'Carly, my wife and I have had nothing to give each other for years but she wouldn't dream of setting me free and I'm eating out my soul for love of you!' But Carly wouldn't accept that. He knew that, and instinctively knew, too, that she would never admit again that she cared for him ... not now, now that she knew he had a wife. That was Carly's code. Other people might behave in an unconventional way and think nothing of it, but not Carly.

On the way back to The Mill House, he and Carly between them filled in about Uncle Fergus and his latest collapse, while Lady Powley's medical man listened gravely. Max sometimes wondered whether this man really liked Lady Powley or whether he was strictly neutral with all his patients. At any rate, he was all that Carly could ask for, when she saw him greet her Uncle Fergus and begin his examination. Numbly she wondered what Guy Morrison would say. Would he agree there had been nothing else to do but to fetch in someone, anyone, or would he think it was because she was embarrassed at his proposal of marriage? She was too

172

weary to think. She and Max listened to what must be done for Fergus and she heard Max say he would put himself and his car at the disposal of the Buckland family. She heard, too, the arrangements being made for Fergus to be admitted to hospital if no change came within forty-eight hours, and undergo extensive tests, probably exploratory surgery. *Who was going to pay for all this?*

She thought wearily of Don Foxwell. He had been a nuisance earlier that day. He had just heard about the proposals for pulling down The Mill House when it was all sold up to the combine.

"And what have I been putting in all this work for, I'd like to know?" he had demanded. "*And* no payment, only promises of future favours!" Carly had been horrified and shocked. Useless to point out that they had given him limitless things they had grown in the garden. He had laughed at her.

Fergus had tottered down the stairs, at hearing Don's raised voice. He was a hefty man, Don; once a labourer, now with his own little business he had built up himself, he had never quite stopped being the truculent type Carly remembered as a child, going up the ladders with a hod of bricks on his shoulder. Now she shivered at the thought, not only of a future married to Don but at the thought of that scene's having upset Fergus, for he must have heard it all. Don had gone, but he would be back.

Max drove away with his wife's doctor, but said he would return with the drugs required for Fergus. Fergus called her to his bedside.

"It's not like you to go to pieces when someone gets a bout of sickness."

She looked dully at him. "I discovered today that Max was Lady Powley's husband. How could I have been so dull-witted as not to know that before?"

Fergus said, "Well, that makes me feel better!" in something like his old voice. "I began to think you were getting like the rest of them, lass, and talked yourself into believing that there was no wrong in being friends with a man who wasn't free. Well, what else could I think? *We* all knew!"

"Why didn't someone say?"

He looked away. "You're a dear girl, but one can't say just what one likes to you, Carly, love. Like your mother in that respect. There is a part of you that is kept secret, well-guarded, and nobody dares to push a way in. Well, that's all right. As it should be. Everyone should be able to keep a part of themselves private and personal. But it's devilish difficult for a poor old guardian like me, who doesn't know much about young women, trying to step carefully yet trying at the same time to do his duty."

"Oh, Uncle, darling, you are a pet, you really are!" she said, throwing herself down beside his bed and hiding her face in his pyjama sleeve.

"Don't cry, for the love of heaven, Carly. I couldn't stand it, the way I feel at the moment. All I worry about is, what's going to happen to you if . . . "

"No ifs, Uncle! Not with horrible Lady Powley's doctor! He has to save everyone — he'd have her to face if he let one of you slip through his fingers. She'd kill his practice, you know she would!"

Fergus tried to laugh and failed. "I don't know. Somewhere along the line I've made a wretched mess of things. I have a career, but somehow my articles aren't all 'taking' — too many rejection slips lately. I keep counting the mouths I must feed, then I recall that you all do a lot to look after yourselves, and that makes me feel terrible. Well, don't look all uppity, my dear. You grow things — but what happens with too many storms like this? There's poor Jay, who dreams of Paris. How can she be told that nothing in the wide world that she can do with her sewing or I can do with my pen will get her that training and career?"

"She might marry," Carly said, then

remembered the row over 'Richard'.

"There's Amy," Uncle Fergus went on. "She wants to train as a vet. Nobody told the child what it would cost and she probably wouldn't be able to comprehend that much money. The future is so simple to a child."

"She might change her mind before she grows up," Carly comforted.

"And Steve. Horticultural college. He couldn't just grow things as you do. He wants a fine career of it. Of course, he's a lad. He's got to have a career. Oh, heavens, what am I going to do?"

"Stop worrying. That sounded like Max's car . . . " and her face flushed rosily and took on a mantle of such beauty that Fergus was still speaking his thoughts aloud without realising it, he was so busy watching Carly's face. "And Holly," he muttered. "Every time she sings, that child reproaches me for neglecting the voice that will probably be more beautiful than even her grandmother's."

Max came upstairs and knocked on

the door. Fergas said, "Let him in. Got something to say to him."

Yet when Max came in, Fergus couldn't say it. How could you ask another woman's husband to look after your beautiful niece, and her young brother and sisters, if you didn't yourself survive? How could a person voice such a thing, anyway, when those two were standing like that? It wasn't that they were looking at each other, or touching hands. They just stood side by side and there was an aura of love that seemed to wrap them so that they were one. Fergus had never seen it before. It embarrassed him. He felt he shouldn't be looking. Of all the things that were said about people being in love, those two really were, and it was a living, tangible thing, and Fergus was frightened, because this was a thing that couldn't be put aside. It would break them first.

The storm raged for two days and so great was the damage and so much was their own G. P. — Guy

Morrison — in demand everywhere, that he hardly seemed to know that Fergus was ill again. Carlotta felt she could stop being quite so tensed. But the worries wouldn't entirely go. And there was the constant presence of Max. Max found Steve looking at his plants and the boy's face struck at him so he started to talk to him.

Max had old tweeds on, a water-stained raincoat that a farmer might have worn and the same sort of heavy boots and dripping tweed brimmed hat. A comfortable person to have around. Steve said, "I don't know what to do. It's not just my own plants: it's Carly's, as well. Those are hers," and he indicated what had been as neat and proficient a kitchen garden as one could wish to see. Rows and rows of prime vegetables flattened by the storm, roots exposed by the water's having washed the soil away. Hours, days, weeks, of patient work all gone to waste. "She does the stuff to sell. She won't be able to pay Don Foxwell now. Oh, lumme,

I've said it. She'll kill me! Don't tell her I told you!"

"But what *have* you told me, that matters?" Max said smoothly. "I've no doubt Foxwell is enough of a countryman to know that this might happen to anyone. Don't worry, lad. Show me your own efforts."

Steve looked up uncertainly into Max's face, and stopped thinking that some grown-ups were dead from the neck up, and accepted that Max knew perfectly well what the inference about Don Foxwell was, and that he would either do some thinking about Carly and the builder at a later date, or else Steve himself had been mistaken and Max didn't really care all that much about Carly. Steve only worried about some things. If he'd had to say what he thought about Max and Carly, he would have shrugged, remarked that with rich people a marriage could become unstuck fairly quickly and easily, if they wanted it badly enough, and thought no more of it. His plants came first.

But now he wasn't so sure. To consider Max in person, one had to take into account that Maxstead Jefferson was not at all like ordinary men. What he would do couldn't be just written off as what everyone else would do. For perhaps the first time, Steve was uncertain and a little afraid. He mumbled, "I grow roses. I'm trying to cross one to get a blue rose. Well, I know it's been done before, but I was daft enough to think I could get a blue rose with yellow linings to the petals." And all the time he was thinking, what will this chap do to our family? If he wants our Carly badly enough, what will he do?

Max said, "Nothing stops, you know, with human beings' experiments. Horticulture, as well as medicine, science, everything, must go forward. You are doing nothing outlandish, you know, in trying to grow a different and quite unusual rose," and Steve, without knowing whether it was Max's tone or the words used, felt so comforted, that he looked up into the dark face above him and blurted out, "What about our Carly, sir?"

Max wasn't the sort to brush aside a lad's question. "In connection with the vegetables, the builder or . . . what?" he asked gently.

Steve drove himself to be brave. "Everything," he said.

"If you had your way, what would happen?" Max put it to him.

Steve was taken aback. "Well, I wouldn't want our Carly to marry that builder chap, not for all the tea in China!" Steve spat out. "And our Carly always pays her debts, and he was shouting at her not long back, and she looked pretty sick. He was wild, of course, because he's done a lot of work on The Mill House, and now he's just heard that Lady Powley's going to . . . " But even Steve couldn't go on. The dark flush of sheer anger in Max's face stopped him, even if his own common sense didn't.

Max said, managing to tamp down

his anger, "What we have to consider first is, of course, your Uncle Fergus and his illness. Have you all thought what you will do if he goes to hospital?"

"He's going to die," Steve said flatly. "Isn't he, sir?"

"Not necessarily," Max said, consideringly. "You see, I believe he has let this thing run on because he was too worried to admit he was ill. Now the normal and next thing will be what is called exploratory surgery. Do you know what that is?"

Steve nodded. "I think so. Cutting a chap open to have a look."

Max chuckled in spite of himself. "What a nice plain way of saying it! Yes, Steve, that about describes it. And of course, there are two things that happen next. Either they can, or they can't, do repair work. I personally believe they will be able to. That's just my opinion, by watching the rather important doctor chap who came to look at your uncle. He's not one to make mistakes, as a rule."

"Who will pay for him?" Steve asked bluntly.

"Well, you're on the way to be a man, and a man has to consider what the cost is of everything. But one of the rules for those who are not yet a man is to remember one doesn't always mention the vulgar subject of money. In your case, you have no reason to worry, even, because it seems that your uncle has some good friends. No, don't get uppity about that. Remember, too, that it is almost always more difficult to receive than to give. Receive graciously, Steve, when the gifts come from the heart."

Steve said bluntly, "If Uncle's got rich friends, how come he's been so beastly worried for years?"

"Because," Max said, looking up at the sky, which had lightened and was not sending down torrential rain but the merest drizzle, "your uncle is a proud man and probably didn't let his friends know he needed them. But they know now, and I think even your uncle will let go of his pride in this special case.

You let go, too, lad, just this once."

He walked away, leaving Steve feeling rather queer. He tried to work out what it was he was feeling and could only think that it was because suddenly he felt as if he had a father again; not a father who sloshed money on horses and laughed with a gaiety that was as false as it was noisy, but a father every boy dreams of. A strong man, giving advice that wasn't hard to take. A big man, one to lean on.

9

FERGUS was taken to hospital in Trowstock. Each one of them, left behind at The Mill House, wondered why that simple fact should have such a weighty effect and train of results that left them rocking. They all knew Trowstock. The hospital was partly the old one, partly the big new extension which Lady Powley had had built on and named after her, for some reason best known to herself. The whole family wished that Fergus could have been taken to the smaller hospital in Fenborough, but then they wouldn't have been able to avail themselves of the services of the best people to look after Uncle Fergus. They naturally took their skills to the superbly fitted new theatres and wards, in the big new extension that had fine views over the surrounding valleys. What Fergus felt about it, they could none of them conjecture, but the rest of the family were thoroughly steamed up.

So, too, was Lady Powley. She had set aside that day for looking at the new bloodstock she was intending to buy, but someone had seen that she heard about her own physician being called to The Mill House and taking Fergus to the part of the hospital she herself had been responsible for building. "And who had that bright idea?" she stormed.

Winters managed to get out of town before she could contact him, and his staff were beautifully blank about what she wanted to know, but Tim Roberts was not so lucky. Lady Powley button-holed him and was determined to have an answer.

Tim wished he had done the same thing as Winters. He had already been over to The Mill House, the moment he had heard about Fergus, but he had forgotten that he had always gone there in the guise of the mysterious Richard.

He blinked and tried to concentrate on what Lady Powley was saying.

It was Max, of course, who had called on her physician, Tim remembered unhappily, so he said, "Why, d'you see, it was a bit of a mess all round. Everywhere flooded in the storms, and their own doctor couldn't be got at, so . . . well, your chap was . . . "

"On hand? What a coincidence! And how come he allowed himself to be taken to that shambles of a place? Surely there was another similar doctor to their own, who could have been called in?"

"Honestly, Lady Powley, I don't know," Tim said wretchedly.

"Where have you been all the morning?" she demanded, suddenly remembering something. "I telephoned around, trying to find you. I want you to come to Jodes' place with me and look at the bay mare."

Tim said, "Actually I was at The Mill House. Well, I'd only just heard — "

"Oh, fine, fine! Well, as you've been

over there in my time, you can regale me with details of what is going on. Go on! What's the matter with the old man?"

"I don't know. I wish I did. I don't think anyone knows. Exploratory surgery, I heard Carly say he was going to have."

"Carly? What sort of a name is that? Sounds like a gypsy! I suppose that's the one everybody raves about!"

Tim nodded. He thought Lady Powley had heard that both Don Foxwell and Keith Anscombe were at each other's throats over Carly's favours. Lady Powley said, "And so my medical man had to be called in, for her relative! Oh, very good! My husband's bright idea, that, I suppose!"

Tim didn't deny it, as she appeared to know about it. Lady Powley thought, Well, we must find a way of making his beauty less desirable to him! "And what particular assets has she, this creature everyone is so mad about? And why do they call her that stupid name, for heaven's sake?"

Tim hadn't been listening. He had been going over the row he and Jay had had, only that morning. He had been beastly to her, he now remembered, when she must have been breaking her heart over the beloved uncle, the same as the others were! He loathed himself. He remembered her screaming at him that she wouldn't be taken for a fool, being told his name was Richard, and given a fancy impression of a man from a rich home, when all the time he was only Tim Roberts, Lady Powley's agent. "What's a name matter?" Tim had asked miserably. "What about your own stupid name, Jay? Why don't they call you something else? They surely must have given you a second name, not just Jewel, of all handles!" and she had exploded again about that. Stupid, stupid, but she had meant it, he thought, when she had sent him away. When Jay said she didn't want to see someone again, she meant it.

He wouldn't admit that the beautiful Jay hadn't got quite the large forgiving heart that Carly had, but the thought was there in his mind.

"Why?" He brought himself back to the question, but he was still thinking of Jay. "Oh, I suppose because she wants to be a concert pianist one day. It's the sort of name a performer might have, I suppose, Lady Powley, isn't it?"

Lady Powley's face was quite white. "They really are getting a bit above themselves, that family, surely; concert pianist, indeed! I suppose they have a grand piano!"

Tim blinked. How did they come to be discussing Jay, for heaven's sake? "No, no, Lady Powley, just an upright, a cottage piano, but it means all the world to her, of course. She practises on it when she can, and she hopes to go to Paris to study . . . "

"Does she indeed. With my husband, no doubt."

Now Tim was angry. "No, Lady Powley, I can assure you, she is *my* girlfriend. I'm sorry if I wasn't there when you rang for me but I'm here now to escort you to look at the horses."

She stormed out, Tim hurrying after her. He was shocked. He didn't know how far the conversation had slipped from his grasp while his thoughts had been with Jay, or how they had got on to the other girl, but the thought of Max even looking at Jay rankled. Yet, he stormed at himself, why should he think that? Everyone knew Max was crazy about Carly. Carly! Heavens, Lady Powley must have been talking about Carly all the time!

He shook his head to clear it and began to form sentences to put to Lady Powley, so that he could clear the matter up, but that wasn't possible now. The Aunt Nerys had arrived and decided she would go with them, and Tim was commandeered to drive the shooting-brake and there was no other chance. He kept his thoughts under control, not even permitting himself to think about Jay in case he slipped up again. Jay would come round, forgive him that stupid masquerade, he was sure. She was just temperamental, like all artistes. She would care much more if something happened to that damned old piano of hers, than that she had been misled by him as to his identity, he thought bitterly.

But in that he was wrong, and it was a full long blisteringly uncomfortable day and evening before he heard what the whole village — Max himself — had heard, that while the whole family had gone to Trowstock to try to be allowed to see Uncle Fergus before his operation, someone had forced an entry into The Mill House and wrecked Jay's piano.

Perhaps only the family and Tim — Max, of course — were upset about it, for that sort of senseless vandalism had happened locally before. The tinker's sons were back and everyone agreed that they would be the most likely to do a stupid thing like that. All Jay's music was scattered around, too, and torn up and nothing was stolen. Not, Carly had to admit, that there was anything very much worth taking. They hadn't even any decent silver any more, thanks to her own father's perfidy where money was concerned and other people's possessions. Carly alone, perhaps, remembered her father taking her mother's last present from her family — a fine silver dressing-table set and brushes — and hocking it for money to put on a horse. How was it that he had only won that one single time, Carly thought distractedly? And what would they do about Jay and the piano — Jay, who made such a noise when she got excited, was simply sitting there among the ruins of it, staring, staring . . .

Max was the only one who could deal with her. He had come over and found everyone in a state of shock. He had taken Jay by the hands and said, "Would *any* piano do, to replace it, or

194

must it be a cottage one? I'm afraid I'm not really musical."

As always, they all stopped making a noise and stared, watching him quietly and efficiently smooth over yet another emotional incident. Jay looked at him, which was something. She had looked through everyone else as if she could no longer see properly. "Are you being funny, Mr Jefferson?" she asked. "I know it was an old one, but it was mine. It was all I had."

"Yes, I know, my dear, and I also know that there is also one that looks like that one did, but is an upright grand. Or you could have a baby grand. I mean, it's possible, if you didn't want a huge grand like the one at Powley Court." And then he caught sight of Carly's face. She was thinking he was boasting again, pretending he had the money to provide another piano. He said desperately, "Of course I don't mean I can *buy* one, Carly," and gave Jay a little shake to keep her attention. "But I know a chap who has a piano and he's away a lot and lets his friends use his flat to keep it occupied but nobody plays the damned thing. Now would you care to practise on it, Jay, for the time being?"

"Are you sure it's all right?" Carly whispered angrily. "You're not just saying . . . " but even she broke off, before the look Max directed at her. She wasn't to know that it had just struck him in that moment, that the tinker's boys wouldn't have come here to perpetrate this piece of senseless vandalism on one item — a piano — and leave everything else intact, unless they had been persuaded. Horrified he asked himself: *would* Isolde to this? And why to Jay? If she had done something to Carly's possessions, it might have made sense.

"Yes, it's all right," he said firmly, and Carly eased out. Jay looked a little less shattered, although of course it wouldn't be like having her own piano. She must tell Richard . . . no, Richard was not really Richard but just plain

Tim Roberts, who was Lady Powley's servant, she thought bitterly. And then she remembered her teacher, that quiet patient but at times forceful man, Edward Yates, who played the organ so divinely and who was trying to keep her own attention on the drier aspects of music lessons when she wanted to be a concert pianist over night. She must ask him what he thought about this. *He* would *know*, she thought, with a little gasp of relief. He was the only one who would know and really understand.

Max said sharply to Carly, "No, don't touch it. Leave everything as it is until the insurance people — at least, I suppose it was insured?" but Carly's distressed face told him, as nothing else could, that it wasn't insured.

"Shouldn't we call the police or something?" Steve suddenly asked, looking at Max, not at Carly. Carly noticed and was surprised. So far Steve had avoided Max.

"I don't believe we will," Max said, thinking. "It will get out, probably get to your uncle, and that would upset him. No, let's clear the mess away, and someone must stay here all the time, even if you take it in turns." He looked at Carly and Jay and frowned. They were, after all, only two girls, with three youngsters to look after. True, they had a dog, but that wasn't enough. They ought to have an older person here with them. "Have you no elderly relative who could come and take charge?" he asked Carly.

"No, there's nobody now, you know. But we'll manage," and she forced a smile that tore at him, because it was such a brave effort and she wouldn't be human if she wasn't a little scared of the responsibility of it all.

"Well," he began, thinking, "if I should remember some older person, someone for instance, who has worked at Powley Court and been retired . . ." and he was trying desperately to make it sound a fortuitous circumstance that such a person should be available when all the time he was thinking of his own old nurse, who was alone and lonely in a small cottage he had managed to get for her before he had gone abroad. But the mention of Powley Court was unfortunate. They all said, in a concerted chorus: "No! No, thank you," but a ring of mulish faces stared back at him.

"All right. But I'll think of something. Meantime try and stay here in a bunch, will you? And lock up before it's dark."

After he had taken himself off, very much preoccupied and afraid to be alone with Carly in case of an overwhelming urge to take her in his arms and comfort her, the rest of them stared in dismay, first at the wrecked piano and music and then at each other. Not until then had they realised how it would be when Uncle Fergus had gone away. He had been in bed unwell before now, but he had been there. In command, the adult, steering their lives, safely. And now they were alone.

That occurred to Max, as he drove

too quickly along the narrow lanes to the town, intent on discovering whether there really was a piano in that flat he had been thinking about. Piano and flat fled before the enormity of his last words to them all. What had he said that for? Well, it had been necessary of course, but it had scared them, at the same time. Now he didn't know what to do for the best.

Caught in a traffic jam, he saw someone waving at him. It was Isolde's Aunt Nerys. He leaned across and opened the passenger door, since she was determined to thread her way through the cars to him. She got in with a couple of seconds in which to shut the door, before the traffic moved at the changing lights.

"You'll kill yourself one of these days," he grinned at her.

"Stop it, Max!" she said wrathfully. "Making me sound so old! Besides, I have been waiting quite a time for you to come along this road and it just occurred to me what a fine fool I'd look if you took the other road. Why didn't you?"

"Well, I would have done in the ordinary way but I suppose I was worried, and not looking where I was going. What's your problem, Aunt Nerys?"

"You, Max! And that trying wife of yours! And that girl you're crazy about! Well, of course you are, or else would you keep going out to The Mill House? Don't look so alarmed — I'm not likely to tell Isolde, much you'd care if I did, come to think of it. But the fact is, she's taken it into her head that it's the pretty one you're after. The one with the outlandish name. Beryl? No, Jewel. That's it! Heard Isolde screaming at Tim Roberts about it today. Didn't sound as if he were really listening to her, the way he was answering," she said, thoughtfully. "Oh, I've had such a time, Max, with Isolde. I went with them — her and Tim — because she was in a terrible temper and he didn't look as if he was going to be much use.

201

Who said that young man was any good with horseflesh, anyway?"

Max waited until they reached the quieter residential roads, then he pulled into the side and shut off the engine. "Now, Aunt Nerys, what on earth are you talking about? What's wrong?"

"Several things," she said roundly. "Isolde's temper gets worse, and she's angry about something big. It can't be that she minds you going off with a pretty girl because she said she doesn't care, but it's something eating at her. Anyway, she set her sights on that black stallion the Colonel is trying to sell. Yes, I know we were supposed to be going over to Jodes' place to look at a bay mare but we ran into the wretched Colonel on the way. His car had broken down and he was making a show of being busy under the bonnet. Fat lot he knows about cars! Then he started talking about that horse of his. The Black Knight or some such stupid name he calls it, and rather cunningly hinted that he didn't think Isolde could hold such an animal. Well, of course, she was furious, and insisted on taking him up with us and going to his place to look the animal over. Would you believe it, she got mounted and managed to keep on the brute for a trial canter round his paddock. And she's going to buy it, what's more!"

Max said nothing.

Aunt Nerys said, "Well, aren't you going to try and stop her?"

"No, I am not," he said quietly. "She'd like me to, I've no doubt, but it wouldn't do any good. And I'm tired of rows with her. I wish to heaven I'd never returned to England."

"I never understood why you did," Aunt Nerys said delicately.

His eyes glinted mischievously. "I'm quite sure you didn't, neither did anyone else," and he let it go.

"Oh, well, I shouldn't pry. I'd like to think you came to get your freedom from Isolde. Not that she'd let you have it, mind you! That would only happen if you made a great show of being afraid she'd get rid of you, leave you adrift with no money and nowhere to get it. No, don't look interested, dear boy — it's too late to pull that one off now, because she's convinced you're interested in one of the girls at The Mill House. The beauty."

Max's eyes widened, but he didn't say anything. Nerys meant well, but she was as garrulous with her friends as she was with him. She didn't even know she was letting secrets out.

But she was on his side, for the moment. "I don't like Isolde," she said roundly, "and I would like to see someone wipe her eye. It isn't fair that one young woman should have everything, and another have so little, and have that little taken away from her. If you don't know the news is everywhere that the musical girl (whichever that one is) at The Mill House has had her piano wrecked, then you're a fool, Max!"

"You know who was responsible, Aunt Nerys?" he asked quietly.

"Oh, everyone does. The tinker's boys, of course," she said blandly, but the way she was looking convinced him that it had been, directly or indirectly, at Isolde's direction. Fury nearly choked him. In that moment, the idea of getting her company interested in something other than the project that wiped out The Mill House was born.

But he said nothing about that. Only the remark that all those young people were now alone, in a house that had been attacked by vandals of whatever persuasion. "I just wish I knew of some reliable elderly person who would be willing to stay with them. I dread the night coming on. Carly's a brave girl, but she's not much older than Jay, after all." And he said 'Carly' as if it were music.

Aunt Nerys forced herself to keep looking at her gloves, so she wouldn't be tempted to pry into his face at that moment. Max was no fool. She said carefully, "Oh, well, we all have our problems. There's you wanting someone to look after that lot, and me trying to find a comfortable berth for my maid, who's really past running about for me, poor thing. You remember Phoebe?"

10

THE Mill House seemed to return to normal, Carlotta reflected, in something like amazement, after the silent but very efficient Phoebe had been installed. Phoebe didn't say whose maid she had been before — she had been warned not to and it wasn't her way to gossip. She just got on with running the place and letting her kindly old eyes rest affectionately on each of them in turn. For her, this was her last move; she now had a family to look after for the rest of her life. She had been told that by Maxstead and she believed him because she worshipped him. The Mill House family, for their part, seemed too distracted to give very much attention to her. Phoebe, aggressively neat and silent, went about things, making them comfortable, almost becoming part of the furniture.

After the way of those below stairs, Phoebe knew the family's business: that Max was no longer in love with his wife and that Lady Powley had treated him shamefully in the past, and still was doing so. Phoebe knew what had happened to the piano and silently absorbed The Mill House family's suspicion and unwilling excitement when a new piano arrived, from a shop in Trowstock, who left the unlikely story that their stock was going into store while the front was repaired after a lorry had crashed into it, and there wasn't room for this little beauty. Jay, who wanted to believe it, did, and sat down and played divinely because she was suddenly happy. Determined to believe that not Max Jefferson but Edward Yates had in a curious way achieved this miracle. Edward had crept secretly into her life, so that now she could even remember without guilt poor Tim Roberts's unhappy face when he learned that she wasn't going to accept his explanation of his absurd impersonation of someone called Richard. It made no difference to her that that was one of his three names. He had, she said roundly, cheated her. She could never trust him again.

Carly thought of Max and wondered what sort of person she herself was. Max, by Jay's standards, had done his share of cheating, even if he hadn't realised it at the time, but Carly couldn't stop loving him. It was like a disease. She now knew the real meaning of heartache. When he came to collect them in a disreputable old saloon car that held them all, to take them to the hospital in the hope of at least one of them being allowed in turn to see Fergus, he stood in front of Carlotta and briefly stared into her eyes, and anyone watching turned away in embarrassment. As Fergus had discovered, what passed between those two was more than a caress. It was almost a fusing of them both, without their bodies moving. Max said, "Hello,

Carly, how are you?" and she said, "Well enough, Max, thank you, and you?" and he nodded. It was the same every time but it hurt the rest of them to hear it. It even worried little Holly, not because she understood what was going on, but because she did understand that the others were unhappy and that her beloved Carly didn't smile any more, now that nice Max Jefferson was here so much.

Every day he arranged something different to keep them all occupied, after the attempt to see Fergus. Sometimes Carly was allowed in to see him, but usually nobody was. Carly was afraid to voice her fears.

One day, alone in the car with Max, after he had dropped Amy at the vet's for a delirious morning in his surgery and going on his rounds with him — a thing Max himself had arranged — he turned to Carly and said, "I know what you're going to ask, my dear, and I'll be frank with you. Even Sir Norbert can't raise much hope at the moment.

Your uncle did allow the thing to run on rather a long time."

She sat staring ahead of her, wrestling with her emotions so that she could manage to thank him for his frankness. But she couldn't and finally he gathered her into his arms and held her, smoothing her hair. They were in the forecourt of the hospital. Ambulances passed them, people passed on their unthinking way — it was nothing new for a person in a car to be wretched and comforted by another passenger. Carly, not a crying person, gave way for yet another time and after she had stopped crying, she thought unreasonably of the first time, down by the bridge, and unfairly blamed Max and his entry into their lives for her misery.

"I never cried before I met you!" she flared. "It's since you came back to this country! Why did you come back? Why didn't you stay abroad?"

It hurt him, though he tried to understand her feelings, but he couldn't tell her the reason. It would have started the old conflict again. He had in fact come back to take part in an amalgamation of two of his companies, those highly successful small companies he had started from the money Isolde's uncle had insisted he should have, so that he didn't have to crawl to Isolde for cash.

"I'm sorry, love," he said. "As soon as your uncle is — well, I'll go away again as soon as I feel I can leave you all."

"Go now!" Carly said bitterly. "Go before . . . before I can't do without you," she choked.

It seemed a long time before Max spoke, but at last he said, as if the words were being dragged out of him, "All right. Perhaps I should. I believe I should have worked that out for myself. I'll leave you all alone anyway."

He drove Carly back to The Mill House and when his car had gone, and the whole countryside seemed to be hushed and waiting for a sound of it returning, Carly realised what she had done and her heart felt like a lump of lead. "But I couldn't do anything else," she told herself miserably. "Not me ... it's not my way," and she trudged into the house.

Edward Yates was there. Carly stopped short and tried to remember who he was, then Jay came through with some sheets of music, her face so happy. Carly could only stare at her. Jay was saying, "Here they are! I knew I had taken them upstairs somewhere and they didn't get torn up like the rest ... " and then she realised that her sister was standing there. "Oh!" she said awkwardly, then with a little rush, "You know Ed — I mean, Mr Yates, my teacher. He came over with some replacements for the music the vandals destroyed. You know my sister Carlotta, I believe?" and her face was steadily going more pink. She looked luscious, like a full-blown rose, Carly thought dazedly, and then with a little rush of sheer gratitude, she found herself thinking, oh, if only that nice man would take our Jay off our hands, we'd never have to see her pining for a musical career and Paris again!

She found Phoebe getting a tray of coffee and homemade cakes to bring in for them. Phoebe didn't say anything but somehow exuded satisfaction, as if she, too, were thinking on the same lines as Carlotta.

Carlotta said, "Stay and have some with us, Phoebe," but received such an eyebrow-raised look that she felt she had committed the worst social solescism possible. After Phoebe had gone out, Jay started to giggle. "Set you down again, Carly? What a shame, and you meant so well!"

"Where did she come from?" Carly demanded wrathfully.

"Why, Edward recommended her, didn't you?" Jay asked him, but he denied it. "Then it must have been the woman in the bread-shop next to the music shop," Jay said comfortably. "Heaven knows, I've shouted in almost every shop there that we needed someone to take over for us."

214

Carly looked angry, an awful fear taking possession of her. She got up and marched out to the kitchen. Phoebe thought she looked exactly as Max's wife should look. She had the presence for it, the upright carriage and justified anger, not the meanness that was so deep-seated in Lady Powley's face. "Who sent you here, Phoebe?" Carly asked quietly.

"A person with your interests at heart, miss," Phoebe said collectedly, "and as I was only chosen provided I didn't betray the source, and as I'm happy here and have nowhere else in the world to go, I would be grateful if you didn't ask me again. It won't help. I doubt if you even know the person who sent me."

So it wasn't Max, Carly thought, with a little rush of feeling she didn't understand. It would be someone who had known Fergus and his secret illness. She nodded, and gracefully apologised to Phoebe, a thing Lady Powley would never do, Phoebe thought with satisfaction.

Carly's aching heart was inclined to blame Max for everything, for taking a hand in every nice thing that happened to them, for now she knew he was Lady Powley's husband, she forgot her old anger when he had said he had money, and now completely believed that everything Max did for them was paid for by Lady Powley however indirectly. That was in her mind when Steve shot into the kitchen the next day. "Hi, Carly, what do you *think*?"

Immediately she furiously asked herself, "What has Max arranged *now*, with the Powley fortune?"

"Tell me," she said, and busied herself with laying trays, a thing that didn't appeal to Phoebe.

"You know I've always wanted to go to Horticultural College?" the boy blurted out and didn't even notice Carly's smouldering anger, because he was looking at Jay walking past the window with Edward, who had brought over more music.

"Yes," Carly said dangerously. "What about it? It's too soon to think about it, anyway. You're only fourteen."

"No, rot!" Steve said, crossly — "Hey, what's that chap doing here again?"

"Mr Yates is being kind to Jay by bringing over bits of music to replace her own that were destroyed when the vandals broke in."

"Oh, yes, that," Steve said, darting his sister an odd look. He had heard several versions in the town about that break-in, and most people seemed to think it had been prompted by someone with a grudge. Carly thought he was looking strange because of Jay with Edward Yates, so she said quickly to side-track him, "Never mind the vandals. Everyone seems to have them at some time or other. What is this about the Horticultural College?"

"Well, you know our head-master?" and as Carly knew him only too well, having attended parent / teacher meetings and stood up to him before now, it didn't really seem to merit an answer, so Steve galloped on, "Well, I saw him in the town and he asked me what I was looking so miserable for, and if I'd given up all my hopes of a horticultural career and when I said no but we couldn't afford for me to go to a decent college — "

"Steve, you never did!"

"No need to get fed up, Carly! Everyone knows we're hard up. Everyone knows about old Lady Powley trying to chuck us out. Anyway, our head said, 'Why on earth didn't your people come and tell me that, boy? I could have arranged something!'"

"Oh, yes? And how come he could be so amenable all at once?" Carly asked icily, but her brother was too filled with the story to notice her manner.

"I don't know. He was waffling on about a junior scholarship thing, but I'd have to take ordinary studies in the morning and horticulture in the afternoons, you know, like Art School scholarships. Oh, Carly, could I, could I?"

"Yes, if it doesn't cost us a penny," she said, then altered it to, "Just a minute, though. Let me think. This doesn't sound right. It'll be that Max Jefferson at the bottom of it."

"Don't be stupid," Steve said, his excitement making him careless of the way he spoke to Carly when she wasn't pleased. "Everyone knows old Lady Powley's got all the money, and it's not likely *she* would do anything for one of us, is it? Everyone knows she hates us because he — " and then Steve caught sight of Phoebe glaring at him from just behind Carly and he pulled up short, red as a beetroot, and fled the room.

"Come back!" Carly shouted, then stopped dead in her tracks. It was true what the boy had said. It must be. And why take away that sheer weight of happiness and excitement in his usually tightly drawn unhappy face?

She turned and found Phoebe behind her. "If I may say so, miss, let it ride. People all around are wanting to help this family. Everyone knows that your uncle is sick in hospital and you're shouldering the burden. Why stop folk being kind, in their way?"

Carly's shoulders sagged, but she jerked herself upright, straight as a ramrod, and held her hands to her face to stop it working. "So long as I can be sure that that woman isn't — I wouldn't take anything from Lady Powley!"

"She wouldn't give anything, miss," Phoebe said dryly. But that wasn't to say that Aunt Nerys, prompted by Max, wouldn't be the power behind that rather involved matter of getting the boy into the life he secretly wanted, without anyone knowing, or even guessing, whose hand was at work, Phoebe thought.

Jay settled, Steve almost settled, Carly realised, going up to her room. Phoebe a tower of strength, there to look after them, to take away the terrifying thought that when darkness cloaked The Mill House, vandals might come again and strike. Carly stood in her room and rested her forehead against the cool of the window-pane and counted the nice things left in her life, against the things that were still rather shakily leaning towards the far from nice. Uncle Fergus and his state of health, for instance. Max, she put out of her thoughts, but he wouldn't be completely banished. Every old car that came up the lane drew her to one window or another, hoping it would be him, until one day Amy came in from her weekly trip to the vet's and said glumly, "The vet dropped me today. That nice Max flew out from Heathrow this morning and nobody knows where he's gone or if he's ever coming back!"

Carly thought she would never be able to go on, after the realisation that Max had kept his word and really gone out of her life. Literally gone out of it — out of the country, as well. But she managed to, if only because the others around her were radiating happiness. Steve lost that pinched look and Jay positively bloomed with happiness. Even Amy smiled more often and when Carly asked her why, and was school more easy to cope with, the child said serenely, "Oh, no, it isn't that. It's because the vet has hinted (only hinted, of course, but I think he really means it) that he might just take me, and see to my training. His wife says he's a good man and he really must be, Carly, because did you know how much it costs to become a vet?"

"Yes, I had an idea, but did you know that you have to go away to veterinary college first?"

"Well, not at first, actually. I mean, you can work *for* a vet, helping him and all that, just to see if you like the work and if you suit, but he says I've got an apti- . . . apti-something for it."

"Aptitude?" Carly said vaguely, looking over the child's head to the far distant tree-tops and thinking that it really must be the vet and not Max who was fixing this because Max was out of the country, and as Phoebe had said, Lady Powley wouldn't give anything or do anything. No, people must be being good and kind because of Uncle Fergus, she thought, with a rush of gratitude. "Don't depend on it, love, but if the thought of it makes you happy, well, I'm happy."

"Happy enough to let me have a pet animal to look after?" Amy asked.

"But we've got a dog," Carly said at once.

"He's the pet of the whole family and also a guard dog. No, I meant a sick animal to look after, of my very own," Amy said, more forcefully than she had intended, because Carly had a sort of manner when she wanted to say 'no', that really didn't necessitate actually uttering that word. You could tell she was going to be against it and would never give in.

Carly was thinking it was the thin end of the wedge. If one sick pet was allowed, several would come. The Mill House was big and rambling and the vet might be thinking it would be a good exercise for the child to have such pets here, supplied by him, because if she was going to get tired of the utter drudgery of looking after sick animals, then sooner rather than later would be best.

But there was no necessity to answer just then for Phoebe called Amy to the kitchen and Carly let her go. But she could hear what Phoebe was saying, all the same, and it made her wonder.

"If I may advise you, Miss Amy, you not having your dear uncle at hand so to speak, it might be a good plan to wait just a bit. I mean, we know very well that The Mill House is not to be taken from you all, after all — "

"How did *you* know that?" Amy demanded. "The vet told me and I was keeping it to tell Carly later."

"I don't rightly remember how I came to hear of it, love, but it's no secret, surely," Phoebe said composedly. "I mean to say, everyone in the village knows that the people who were going to buy all this land to make a holiday place of it have suddenly lost interest and gone somewhere else in the neighbourhood. That way, folk around here aren't upset, on account of the work it'll provide still being around, but it won't be just about here so The Mill House won't be taken away."

"Funny thing, isn't it, for people to change their minds like that?" Amy asked crossly, caring more for everyone else knowing something she thought was her bit of hot news.

"Well, I always wondered why they did want this swampy land," Phoebe said. "But who's to say what business gentlemen think they'd like? One thing I *do* know, it'll perhaps make your uncle get better more quickly, now he knows he doesn't have to lie in hospital a-worrying about where you're all going to go, if things move too quickly here before he can get out. I mean, did any of you think of where you'd be living, if you had to leave here?"

"Yes," Amy said in surprise. "In the house Lady Powley promised to find for us."

"Oh, that," Phoebe said, in such a tone as to make the listening Carlotta realise that she hadn't been the only one to distrust the promise of alternative accommodation. She let out a big sigh of sheer relief that they weren't going to have to move, yet at the same time she experienced disappointment. The Mill House needed, really needed, that constant attention Don Foxwell had been giving it and now he was too angry to come near the place.

She forgot Don Foxwell and the fact that the roof was starting to leak in a new place, for news came that Fergus was to have his surgery. It blotted out everything else. Phoebe said, "I shouldn't wonder if they knew this was coming up, miss, and didn't let you all know, so that you wouldn't be worrying yourselves. Now, in a few hours, we'll perhaps have some good news. And I think it would be a very nice idea if we were all to go out for the day. Have a picnic somewhere. What do you all say?"

"Oh, Phoebe, I couldn't," Carly said, and the others said so too, in different ways. Little Holly just burst into tears, and threw herself against Carly, in a way she hadn't done for a year or two. "Uncle's going to die, isn't he?" she sobbed.

"No, love, we don't know that," Carly said, smoothing her hair, then looking at Phoebe, she said, "Well, I suppose it might be a good idea if we all did something different, but not a picnic. Too much time to think. How would it be if we were to go into the town . . . "

"How?" Steve asked bluntly. "We've only got the one bike."

"Well, bus, I thought," Carly said mildly.

"Well, I don't want to go," Steve said. "If I do anything, it's to dig over that new patch and try a bit of an experiment. I don't get much chance of gardening lately, one way and another."

Phoebe said, "Well, I shall be staying here, of course. It will be a good chance to turn out some cupboards."

"If I stay with you," Holly said, wiping her face on Carly's dress, "would you make me some gingerbread men?" and Phoebe promised she would.

"But," she added, "I would really like *you* to go into the town, miss," and she looked hard at Carlotta. "Miss Jay's with that nice Mr Yates, and Amy wants to wait for the vet to pick her up. You'll be the only one with the same old things to do, and it's not good for you. Besides, there's a thing or two I'm needing from the shops."

"But I want to be here for when the hospital rings up," Carly protested.

Phoebe looked at her and Carly realised she was wanting Carly alone to go into the town and wait at the hospital, without the others hearing, or they would all want to go. And if things were not to go the right way, it would have to be Carly who would be the one to be there. "No, I see that isn't practical," she said quickly. "Okay, Phoebe, give me a list of what you want."

The bike had been repaired, after its last adventure the day Carly had gone for the doctor for poor Fergus. Someone had paid for it. There was no sense in hammering at Will at the service station, for he had repeatedly said he had repaired it in return for a favour Fergus had done him. Carly knew that wasn't true.

She was just going round to the shed for the bike when the postman came. More rejections of poor Fergus's work, she supposed, automatically holding out her hand for the large envelopes of returned MS.

"Not rejections today, miss," the postman said cheerfully. Everyone knew your business in Cheltonwood. "Looks like these small ones might just hold a cheque or two, eh? Going to the hospital? Nice surprise for your uncle!"

11

CARLY took them and turned them over. One had the newspaper's name across the top. It was the biggest local and would probably pay well. The other one was an even larger provincial daily.

Carly took them in and went upstairs to Uncle Fergus's desk, to put them with other mail that had come for him. They weren't allowed to let him see his mail for fear of upsetting him. She put them on the pile of other letters, and it struck her that they were almost all small envelopes, and almost all with the same local newspaper on the top.

She closed the desk and went downstairs. "Phoebe, do you happen to know the local office of The Star and Chronicle?"

Phoebe was busy at the oven and always seemed distracted when trying cakes to see if they were done. Unthinking, she said, "Those two old has beens? Oh, well, I suppose I shouldn't say that, seeing as they've both been taken over and put together and a lot of money pumped into them, should I?"

Carly's heart began to beat faster. A doubt that had started up in Uncle Fergus's room began to blow itself up in size and she said in a hushed voice, "They wouldn't have had Lady Powley's money pumped into them, I suppose?"

But now Phoebe had finished with the oven, to her satisfaction, and could give her thoughts to what her errant tongue was doing. "Hardly, miss," she said, and even managed a smile. "What would Lady Powley want with local newspapers?"

"To make more money, like trying to take this house from us?"

"Oh, no, miss, Lady Powley's interested in big business and horseflesh and not really much else," Phoebe said tranquilly.

Carlotta let her breath out in a long sigh. "Then Uncle Fergus's work must be making good on its own," she said, half to herself, and didn't notice the sharp look Phoebe gave her.

She took the bike into Trowstock and gave a great deal of thought to those letters. She should be opening them and acknowledging them, she supposed, and paying the money into the bank, if there was money in them. If only Max were still here, he would be able to tell her what to do. Uncle Fergus was so used to getting his work rejected that he hadn't briefed her what to do about acceptances.

She called at the hospital to find out what time they would hear any news, but was told vaguely that nothing could be said definitely, so she went to look at the offices of The Star and Chronicle. It used to be in an alley off the High Street, a shabby shop window with photos of local events pinned to a baize board behind the glass. Now she saw that that had all gone and the paper was housed in the building recently finished, on the main road. A brassy-looking black-and-silver modern structure, so lush and spick and span that she lost her nerve and abandoned the idea of going in to try and see the editor herself.

What could Fergus have possibly written, to be accepted by this new company with all the material they would have pouring in, she asked herself, with a frightened little flutter. She had heard the old editor say once to Fergus, on the telephone (his voice being the booming kind that could be heard by other occupants of the room), that he was sorry, he would have liked to take Fergus's articles which were good sound stuff, but not world-shaking enough for his paper. He was in such circumstances that he had to take unusual stuff to sell the paper at all. So what was happening now?

She wished Jay hadn't gone off with Edward Yates, but he had kindly decided to keep Jay's thoughts off the beloved uncle and got time off to take her out for the day. Carly absently wandered into Woolworth's, and three other big stores, buying nothing, not even actually seeing the goods on sale, until she was brought up short by the sheer familiarity of some things on the counter: mugs and plates, with her own characters on them — Mack and Jack. She stared unbelieving. There was the country scene, the little boy and the cheeky dog, and as her eyes roved the counter, she saw that a whole range of pottery — egg-cups to jugs and soup-bowls, were carrying the same characters, the same scene. And above, there was a poster urging people to buy the very latest and favourite characters.

It was the picture she had given to Max, she recalled. Anger rose in her, to think he would do this, then puzzlement took over. *How* had he done this? How could a person knowing nothing about an artist's work market and launch it on *things*? Was it true what he had said, about owning an advertising agency? The thought was swept from her mind as she passed a window showing children's play clothes, and there were Jack and Mack on the front of tee-shirts, the pockets of children's shorts, even on babies' bibs and feeding garments. And then her heart turned right over, as she saw her own reflection in the shop window, and the man standing by her side.

Somehow she forced herself to turn round and look up at him. "*Max!*" She gasped his name. "You're *back*!" and all thought of her anger fled.

"No. I never went away," he said. "Did you think I'd leave you until we knew how your uncle was?"

"But you said . . . And someone else said you'd flown out from Heathrow and there didn't seem any reason to not believe it . . . "

"Oh, that! Just a short business trip to Paris and Bonn. Apart from that, I've been here all the time, my dear, and I *didn't* want you to discover about this before I could tell you, only somehow there wasn't an opportunity and then . . . I'm afraid I forgot."

He had forgotten because he had also been in London arranging two very large business deals, but again he didn't feel he could tell Carly, remembering her anger when he had mentioned big business before.

"You forgot!" Her own anger rose swiftly. "I expect you forgot you didn't even ask my permission to do this?" she stuttered.

"You might have refused it," he said, smiling broadly. "One never knows what you'll do or say next, Carly."

He wasn't hers and his presence there, making light of what he had done with her poor little drawing, incensed her even more than it would have otherwise done. "What did your wife say to the deal? Or was it with her consent too?" she flared.

It certainly wiped the jolly smile from his face. He said, "I don't know what she thinks about it. I haven't seen her since the day before I last saw you,

Carly. I told you, I had finished with her and she refused me my freedom so that was the end of it."

"You make it sound so simple!" she said indignantly.

"Simple it may be, but that doesn't mean it makes me any happier. Not when I see you unhappy and I am powerless to change things for you."

"Oh, and how do you think you could change things for me?" she asked, fanning the flame of her anger so that she shouldn't dissolve into tears again. "We are doing very nicely. Uncle's well enough to have his surgery — today! And he's now having acceptances and not rejections, so his work can't be so bad. And Steve has had the chance of a scholarship to Horticultural college and Amy seems to have convinced the vet that she's prime material for an apprentice and Jay has . . . "

Something in his eyes stopped her. It was difficult to pin down what it was but she found herself thinking that this was not news to Max.

He said quickly, before she had time to gather her thoughts together, "I believe it might be in order to call at the hospital to see if there is any news, don't you, Carly, and while we're on the way, there's something I want to tell you."

"Not about you being rich!" she was goaded to say.

He seemed surprised. "No, actually I was going to say that your uncle has heard that nobody wants to take the house from you all, but I was a little puzzled to learn that he seemed rather bothered. Can you explain that, Carly? I thought he didn't want to leave the house.

"No, he doesn't, but perhaps he's a little sharper than I am, at putting two and two together. Did you have a hand in changing Lady Powley's mind?"

"My dear, I told you, I have had no contact with her, nor am I likely to. And believe me, I am quite incapable of changing her mind about anything so I wouldn't try," he said, with such truth that Carly was forced to believe it.

They were told to wait, but not brusquely. Carly said sardonically, "It must be your influence, the way they speak to you. They didn't tell me in that tone that there was no news."

The porter heard her and grinned. "Well, miss, that's because — " he began, but caught Max's wrathful look, muttered, "Sorry, sir," and walked sharply away.

"What was all that about?" she demanded.

"I do not like familiar staff," he said coldly, and Carly decided that must be the reason, and subsided. Suddenly she was no longer angry, just scared.

Fergus wasn't down from theatre yet. Max seemed to know several people here. He chatted to a competent-looking man who turned out to be the Hospital Secretary and then he was invited to take tea with Matron herself. He took Carly down. "In this hospital they still say 'Matron'," he grinned, "and they haven't heard of the Salmon System."

239

Matron's room looked out over a pleasant little bit of garden. She was youngish. Carly had always thought of the Matron of a hospital as a comfortably round person. But this one was certainly as efficient and confident as Carly had expected. And she liked Max.

Tea was served, while she told Carly with a half smile that one of the surgeons had come out of theatre looking rather pleased. His part of the job was over. It was a longish operation. "I've been reading his articles, Maxstead," she remarked, passing a plate of biscuits to Carly, who refused them. She couldn't have eaten anything to save her life. "Fergus is good! Why wasn't he discovered before? Oh, well, I suppose now you've gingered that lot up, it will — " and then her eyebrows shot up in interrogation. Carly hadn't been looking at Max, so she didn't see the reason for the Matron's sudden cutting off what she was saying.

Max said smoothly, "I have always found that no matter how people plug away at something that means something to them, it doesn't come to fruition until the time Fate decreed it would do. If Fergus is having a success now, it simply means it wasn't meant to, before. Like Carly's sister, Jay. That girl is breaking her neck to become a concert pianist. I consider she plays divinely, but I do wish I could have the temerity to urge her to stop breaking her heart over the slowness of achieving her heart's desire."

Matron looked interested in his speech but Carly was surprised. It wasn't like Maxstead to talk like that. She tried to pull her thoughts together and found herself saying, "I don't think Jay will be so eager to jump before she can run, not now she's discovered her teacher is nice as a man."

"Oh, like that, is it? Well, that's fine," Maxstead said.

Carlotta was still not watching him. Her thoughts were on her uncle. "What will he be like, if . . . when he comes through this operation?"

"Good girl!" Matron noticed and approved the changing of 'if' to 'when'. "A lot depends on himself. He'll have a long haul back. Have you made any arrangements for convalescence?"

Carly said, "No," rather blankly, and Max said at the same time, "Yes." They both looked at him and he continued, doggedly, "Well, I like him, Carly, and I know the surgeon rather well, and we consider Fergus should go to some warm place, such as the Canaries."

Carly said distinctly, "You must be out of your mind. Money, Max. We have none."

"Oh, dear, love, you are obsessed with that nasty little five-letter word. Who cares about money? The thing is, he has a great admirer who happens to have a house in the Canaries and has said . . . "

"Oh, no!" Carly got to her feet. "You're doing it again, Max. You were rich, not so long ago, then you changed your mind and said you'd got an advertising agency. Max, when will you stop romancing and remember I'm a very down-to-earth person? We can't afford convalescence anywhere for my uncle. He'll have to come back to The Mill House."

Matron was saying nothing, but watching them both closely. When Carly had risen to her feet, Max had also risen, and like Fergus on that other occasion, Matron became aware of the situation between them. To cool the atmosphere between them, she said mildly, "Or the hospital's own convalescent home in Somerset. Very sheltered and mild there, usually," and at that moment the telephone rang, so they both politely sat down again while she answered it.

Carly felt sick. It would be to say that Fergus hadn't made it. She was sure of it. She thought of the house at Cheltonwood without Fergus. It had been bleak enough while he had been away in hospital, with Phoebe in charge, but what if he were never to come back again?

Matron replaced the telephone and looked pleased. "I asked them to ring me as soon as they were finished. They have, and he's going to be all right."

Carly felt a buzzing in her ears. She looked odd and Max wasn't listening to Matron. Matron decided she had something to say to someone in the outer office and left them. Max wordlessly gathered Carly into his arms, murmuring to her, "It's all over. It's all over, and it's all right, love. All right."

Fergus made strides. Carlotta, sitting beside his bedside, marvelled at the way his voice had changed; stronger, with interest alive in his eyes. The hospital was within reach of The Mill House, with the old bicycle, and Fergus spent a lot of time on one of the balconies, his portable typewriter on a small table, his notepad by his side.

"They don't let me do too much typing at a time," he admitted ruefully to Carlotta, "but every day I feel a little better. Every day I am given more latitude, though Matron is such a bully."

Carlotta eased out a little inside, but she found it impossible to be completely contented. Something was wrong somewhere.

"You don't have to keep things from me now, my dear," Fergus said suddenly to her, one day some weeks after his operation. "You're bothered about something. What is it?"

She made a helpless gesture with hands and shoulders, almost a Gallic shrug. "I'm ungrateful, darling. Everyone's been so kind, and yet . . . "

"And yet . . . what? Tell me, everything. You know about Maxstead, and that wife of his, and you don't seem to be bothered about that. I can tell, because you don't look at him with loathing now, when you both meet," and he half smiled. That was worrying him more than he cared to admit.

"Did I look at him with loathing?" She was surprised. "Oh, well, it was that boasting of his, that he was rich. I see now why. It was his wife's money that he had."

She was frowning down at the floor as she spoke, so she missed the start that Fergus gave. So she still didn't know everything! Why hadn't Max told her of his success? As a self-made man (financially) he appealed very much to Fergus. Maxstead's good nature had been taken advantage of in the past by so many people.

"Does it matter, my dear?"

"Well, yes, it does. At first I thought he was the person fixing us all up, then common sense told me that he was too hard up to be the one so it had to be his wife's money, but right away I saw that wasn't possible. She keeps a tight hold on the purse-strings. But, Uncle Fergus, *someone* is fixing us up. Someone persuaded that beastly headmaster of Steve's to tell him he could go to horticultural college on a scholarship. Steve thinks it will be soon. I haven't the heart to tell him he must wait till he's at normal school-leaving age."

"Maxstead has told him. I've seen him today, and he's been so good to the boy, within his limited means. He knows a small market-gardener who could use Steve at week-ends, pay him, and teach him, which will settle the lad until anything else comes up."

Carlotta flushed. "Why should another woman's husband do that for us?"

"Because he has no happy home and wants a share of ours," Fergus said simply. "He's been so kind, with effort, having no money. I don't begrudge him the enjoyment of our family."

"Well, I do!" Carlotta choked. "Okay, I'm sick and silly over him. You must know that. I'm deeply ashamed, but I love him and want him and I hate myself for it. He's not mine to have, and I want him to go away but he won't. *Someone* has arranged for Amy to be settled at the vet's surgery in the week-ends. She's only a child and she's aware of nothing wrong. And that piano of Jay's — nobody, but nobody, is going to convince me that that shop in Trowstock that got smashed in with a crashing lorry just happened to be without enough storage space for one grand piano and said they were glad to have someone like Jay use it, in her own home. No, Fergus, that's too much!"

Now he looked worried, so she said, "Oh, I shouldn't have told you. I've set you back!"

"No, no, my dear, not at all. I must know about the family, and all I can say is, if it makes everyone happy to have a little help to further their gifts, what's wrong with that?"

"The ethics of it, of course!" Carlotta said indignantly.

He sighed. He knew Max had bought the piano for Jay. It had given Max pleasure to do so. Where was the harm in that? He knew it was Max's money paying the surgeon for his work on Fergus. Max loved Carly and had no other way to show it. Besides, Fergus had suffered too much pain to care overmuch how he got his surgery. It was pure heaven to know that he was cured and it was pure heaven to know that his little family were getting help with their talents. Everyone except Carly appeared to be happy and Carly was nearest his heart. He looked distressed and she said contritely, "Oh, Uncle darling, look what I've done! But you did ask me — you did want to know what was going on, and you didn't seem too upset when they told you how Jay's piano was wrecked."

"No, because you've got someone with you all the time. I would have worried about vandals if you'd been alone in charge of the family. This Phoebe, I never did hear how you found her."

12

DOUBT pricked Carly again. "Well, Jay seemed to think it was through her telling everyone in the shops near the church that we wanted someone. She won't take any money, though. She says it's enough to have a family to dote on, and her room and board."

Fergus smiled and patted her hand. "Then that's fine. It restores my faith in human nature," but he wasn't so happy in his mind. He, too, had asked himself why vandals should attack a piano and music, and nothing else, and how it was that such an acceptable person as Phoebe should appear and not want remuneration. Maxstead again? They were getting too much in his debt.

"Of course, it could have been Jay's music teacher," Carly said suddenly. "Edward Yates, you know. He's seeing a lot of Jay lately, and I get the feeling that they like each other specially." She looked anxiously at Fergus. "Would you be happy if — "

He sighed. "More than happy. Jay is too pretty to be fancy-free and Yates is a very sound man. But you, my dear girl, what will you do with your life? They tell me you've managed to persuade someone to market your little characters in the picture you did."

Carly nearly choked with fury. "Who told you?" she demanded. "Not Max, surely? He did! I can see it in your face! Oh, it's too much. He asked me once if he could do something about it. I said no. He happened to see the picture I put in . . . well, in Mother's room. He did rather press to show someone the picture, so I thought I'd spike his guns. I sent it to him as a present. Uncle, what sort of a man uses a gift to make a commercial thing of it? It's everywhere, so soon, too," and she told him where she had seen it. "And how could it have happened? Even I know a person needs to have money to launch a thing like that. If he used that wife's money to do it . . . "

"The work has to be good to make a popular sales gimmick," Fergus said slowly. Why had Maxstead launched Carly's work without telling her, for clearly he had done it. Who else would have done it? "Carly, I lie here thinking of you all. Foxwell, what about him? How has he taken the news about The Mill House being pulled down, after all his work on it?"

"But it isn't going to be pulled down, darling. We're not to leave the place. Didn't you know? I thought you did. The people who wanted to buy the land from Lady Powley have gone off the idea.

Now he looked really worried.

"But you didn't want to leave The Mill House. Aren't you pleased, Uncle?" Carly frowned.

"It must have escaped your notice, my dear, that I have the interest of all of you at heart, and it came to my notice that you all wanted to leave the place. Now we're stuck with it."

"Well, nobody could persuade the combine to go off it, could they?" she reasoned.

Lady Powley wasn't so easy to persuade. At that moment she had contacted the firm, having failed to find Maxstead. She was told that it was her husband who had swayed them towards a more desirable property in the district, and they had been assured she wouldn't mind all that much.

"Not mind! All I need is to see The Mill House razed to the ground, and something useful and commercial in its place," she gritted.

"There is now a doubt that it would have made such a success. Not such a success as the Seven Acres property," the smooth male voice assured her "But that isn't my property," she said, angrily.

"Well, it's your husband's, so it's all in the family, isn't it?" he murmured, and sounded puzzled. "We have been assured it's acceptable to you, Lady Powley."

"Have you indeed?" she said, slamming the telephone down. Max! So it was true, the rumours she had heard, that he was no longer needing her money. It might even be true that Max was the owner of certain new firms she had been unable to buy her way into, such as that new mushroom lot producing the gimmicky Jack and Mack. It might even be true, the rumour that that girl who had caught Maxstead's eye was really the artist who did those things. She recalled that the mother had been something of an artist, too.

She strode up and down, itching to do something; something to hurt Jay, who still figured largely in her mind as the one Max was interested in. Hurt Jay and hurt Max through her. How deeply had it bitten, that she could no longer snap her fingers and get Max back? To think he had told her he wanted his freedom and would take it, with or without her consent!

Furiously she changed into her riding-kit and went down to the stable — a good hard ride might help. That great black horse she had unwisely bought off the Colonel was doing his best to kick out yet another loose-box door. Already she had lost two good stable-hands. They just hadn't the nerve to work with the great beast. Well, she would show the animal who was master around here.

Isolde in a temper was a force to be reckoned with. Her crop chastised the animal and he in turn kicked her, catching her enough to throw her across the stableyard but not enough to break any bones. Angrily she got up and mounted him, stuck to him though he reared and tried to throw her, and finally she got him under sufficient control to walk him out. Her anger wouldn't let her give him the reins, for a good gallop over the open countryside. She forced him to walk through the traffic of the town. Lathered, his eyes rolling whitely, he was held in check among traffic by the hand of someone he had to acknowledge — however temporarily — as his master. But the Black Knight wasn't an animal to forget that easily.

He almost had her off his back in a moment when her concentration was taken by the sight of Jay, hanging on to a man's arm, looking up into his face with a smile of sheer beauty. The man was half hidden by other pedestrians in that quick glance, Isolde's attention taken up almost entirely by Jay — her lovely face and figure, her smart clothes which didn't appear to be home-made. Isolde jumped to the conclusion — a conclusion she wanted to jump to — that it was Maxstead with the Buckland girl. Maxstead playing a favourite game, pretending to be just like other men, strolling with a young woman through the town. Her anger almost choked her and, confusing the one who had the gift of drawing 'Jack and Mack' — those two favourite characters that were obvious in almost every shop in the High Street — Isolde decided to mete out a little more punishment.

But not via the tinker's boys; they had all most inconveniently but predictably moved on, at least until the 'vandalism' to Jay's piano died down a little. No, Isolde must do this job herself: casually, neatly, and no evidence of her own hand in it. Who would think that Lady Powley, of all people, would openly ride over to the house at Cheltonwood and damage the sketches in the studio, in broad daylight?

Not until it was done would she give the Black Knight his head either, she promised herself. She held him in on a tight rein, taking a field path, then dropping down into the lane which ran towards The Mill House. The Black Knight couldn't understand it. This was open land, for a gallop, but he was still on a tight rein. So he minced quietly along, in a way that should have warned Isolde, and made no sign of his mounting restiveness.

At the top of the rise, she had a brief but good view of The Mill House and saw Amy, Steve and little Holly run out, calling to someone behind them. It wouldn't be the musical girl — Isolde had just seen her in the town, hadn't she? It might be the other girl. Isolde didn't know Carlotta was at the hospital, talking to her uncle. But the person coming out behind the children with a picnic basket and a rug was one she knew well — Phoebe, that tiresome maid Aunt Nerys had just pensioned off. What on earth was she doing here? More of Maxstead's conniving? Or was Aunt Nerys a traitor to Isolde, too?

Now she could hardly see clearly for the anger that rose in her. The need to hurt someone was blinding. She waited for the little party to cross the stone bridge and make for the flat picnic spot, then she gave the Black Knight his head, jumped the mill-stream and came to a sudden halt in the yard at the back. The big horse pulled up extremely unwillingly, while Isolde still held on to the rein.

The place was shut up and deserted. They were all out and there was the studio. She could see through the big windows. The studio — built against the side of The Mill House — was Carlotta's refuge. In times of stress, even in the middle of the night, she had come there and sketched those vivid lightning pictures of the people she knew, those who meant most to her. Isolde tethered the horse and walked round, staring in the big windows, at the drawings standing against the walls.

There was a picture of the beauty, playing the piano (the old one that Isolde had caused to be destroyed), and in her face was a passion for music that was frightening. Each of the Bucklands was there, with an economy of line that was revealing and surprising. Who had this surprising talent? The one who had done the sketch a commercial firm had taken up: 'Jack and Mack', which had caught on so suddenly and become so popular. And which clever person had swamped the market with those goods, at low prices that were a sure sell. Not Maxstead? Now thoughts were racing round in her mind, about his interest in this family, as she glared at a sketch of young Amy with a marmoset in her arms, and another of Steve almost reverently taking up a delicate plant from a compost pot, holding the roots as a good gardener would, rapt in his attention so that he clearly had no idea he was being sketched. But no picture of the one who was doing all this.

Who was it? Which one? Somehow in that moment Isolde knew there must be someone else here who was captivating Max. The girl who had the town by the ears, the one who was not good-looking but who captivated everyone, male and female alike? So it was said. Isolde didn't believe such a person could have such a power, but at the same time, now that she thought about it, she was pretty sure that it would take more intelligence than the family's beauty to captivate and hold Isolde's husband.

She untied the horse and remounted him. He didn't like it and tried to throw her again, so she lashed out at him and sent him tearing up the slope. A good run cross-country would settle him, she thought, and it might clear her own mind as to what she should do. Hurt Max, and hurt the girl who had stolen him, but which one was it?

As the wind tore through her hair, she felt an overwhelming hatred of all the Buckland family, who seemed to take the whole of Max's interest. She had heard how much time he spent at The Mill House, with the whole family. Her uncles had told her once, as a child, that she must learn that great wealth meant nothing. It was merely a thing that a person possessed, but could lose, to another person. These Bucklands had no money at all, but they had so many other things, things which her uncles would have admired because they, too, had not possessed them. And they had liked Max, who had no money at all and no hopes in the world of a title, though there was one in his family. And Max, it seemed, had discovered a talent for business, if the rumours could be believed.

On the road below, she noticed the blue-and-red striped van belonging to Don Foxwell, heading towards The Mill House. Don Foxwell, one of the men who had thought he was going to marry the plain Buckland girl. Isolde turned the horse's head in that direction and guided him down the slippery slope towards the road, to head off the builder in his lorry. The Black Knight didn't like this treatment at all, but Isolde's hands held him firmly to her will.

Don Foxwell saw her coming. He was still smarting over the treatment he had received from Carlotta, the last time he had tried to force his attentions on her. He still couldn't see how she had held him off. That cool manner of hers, the way she lifted her eyebrows and looked at him, had made him feel quite unaccountably small, yet who was Carlotta Buckland to play the high and mighty madam with him, almost like Lady Powley herself? He was torn in two. He wanted Carlotta, because of the work he had put into The Mill House and because, without looks, she managed to cut him down to size and keep him in his place. Yet surely that uncle, who hadn't a bean, would be glad to see her married off? He had his work cut out, surely, to feed and educate that lot, *and* all this fancy surgery to pay for?

With one eye on Lady Powley approaching, and remembering the way she, too, had rebuffed him, the last time he had asked for a chance to do some work at Powley Court, he slowed his van down.

Lady Powley showed off her prowess with tricky horses, by pulling up and staying on the great beast's back as it reared high above the van. Don Foxwell nervously hoped she'd keep it away from his vehicle and when she pulled back, he got out and stood by her.

"Well, Foxwell, I've been thinking about you and the work at the Court," she said coolly, "but I suppose you've got too busy since we spoke of it?"

He seethed. Considering she had hardly been polite to him and almost thrown him off her property, that really was the limit. But he needed the prestige, as well as the work, so he said, "Never too busy to do anything for you, Lady Powley."

"Glad to hear it!" she said. "Going to marry the elder Buckland girl, I hear?"

Don Foxwell's face was a study. Was she pulling his leg, since everyone knew, to his acute discomfort, that neither he nor Keith Anscombe had got anywhere with Carlotta, and moreover, didn't she know Carlotta was playing around with Lady Powley's own husband?

"That is the intention," Don Foxwell said, his emotions mixing madly in his heavy over-red face. "Can't seem to make up her mind to say yes, but she will, though. That uncle'd be glad to get her off his hands, I'm thinking, and to someone who'd be of use around the property, now it seems it's not to be taken away from them," he added slyly, looking speculatingly at Lady Powley. Like a good many other people, he would have given a lot to know just how Lady Powley's plans had been overset and the Bucklands left peacefully in the house at Cheltonwood.

Lady Powley kept her countenance and said carelessly, "Oh, well, up to you to pull it off, Foxwell. Marry the girl and there'll be regular work for you at Powley Court. Can't have anyone working for me whose attention is distracted by his young woman being uncertain."

"She's never at home," he said bitterly, wondering how he could phrase words that would convey subtly that Carlotta was elsewhere with Lady Powley's husband. The work at the Court was in the balance and Lady

Powley was a tricky customer to deal with.

"Oh, don't make excuses, man. She's in now — saw her. In the studio. Don't take any notice of locked doors — have a bit of grit and face up to her. You want the girl, be a man and make her say yes. It's up to you."

He watched her take off again, lashing the horse up the slippery slope of the field again. All his anger against Carlotta rose to mingle with the strange reality of Lady Powley literally pointing the way to his forcing entry into the studio at The Mill House to make Carlotta agree to marry him. As he drove along the bumpy road, he decided what he would say to Carlotta, his thoughts coloured by the picture Lady Powley had painted of a bright future with permanent work at Powley Court. For the moment, he had forgotten the firm of contractors who usually did everything there, and remembered only that Lady Powley had talked to him.

At the top of the rise Lady Powley

kept the big horse still with difficulty while she watched the tiny figure of the burly builder leave his van well beyond The Mill House boundaries and walk back, lighting a cigarette as he went, no doubt to boost his confidence. Let him, she thought with satisfaction, be the one to smash his way into the studio, and no doubt vent his spleen on the pictures and sketches, when he found the girl wasn't there. Lady Powley had no doubt that the down-to-earth Foxwell would consider sketching, in a wife, an undesirable gift.

He seemed to be there some time. Her curiosity overcoming her, she quietly rode down again. Not a thing was moving, anywhere. No sound of the builder smashing up the studio.

He had lost his anger, because he had found a picture of himself. Carlotta had put him on to paper, with the minimum of lines, while his back was turned towards her. He stared at it. Was that what he looked like? He stared at the brute strength in his muscles, yet he could see how Carlotta had captured his love of his work, easing in a shaped brick, slickly filling between the cracks with mortar. He was good at his work and Carlotta had put it all on paper, with such a few strokes. He couldn't understand it. But what sort of wife would a woman be, who had this extraordinary gift? It had half frightened him, half irritated him. He must think. She was not here now, even if she had been here recently, and he supposed he'd have to come back and make good the damage he'd done, forcing his way in. He threw down his cigarette end, too put out to remember to crush it under his heel. He didn't see Lady Powley easing the horse down through the trees, to see what was keeping him. He went through the back, taking a short cut to where he had left his van, so Lady Powley didn't see what happened to him. It was all so quiet, her curiosity consumed her.

It was at that moment that the van started up, with a roar, disturbing the quiet of a country afternoon. It startled the horse and the flare of flame that shot up suddenly from the dropped cigarette and catching light to oily rags and the contents of a fallen bottle of white spirit finished it. The horse took off and she couldn't hold it. Behind her, the studio was going up in flames, the tinder-dry contents burning with ferocity, but Lady Powley was unaware of it. She fought to keep on the back of the sorely tried Black Knight, but he finally managed to throw her, breasting a familiar rise that led down to his previous home, the property of the Colonel, who later found Max's wife's body, flung against a low stone wall like a discarded rag doll.

That afternoon Carlotta had left her uncle, feeling distinctly miserable. Impending disaster, the family had always called the feeling. But why should she feel like that? Fergus was so much better and she couldn't help noticing how the Matron's name had crept into so many remarks he had made. Apparently they had known each other for some time, though he had never mentioned it.

Carly went into the local park and sat down to do what, from childhood, had been a good way of sorting one's thoughts: counting one's blessings. But it wouldn't work. When she thought of Jay's ripening friendship with her music teacher, it just made her heart ache to think that Max would never be free for her. When she thought of Amy holding the little monkey, she recalled that the child was still asking for permission to have sick animals at The Mill House and she had forgotten to speak to Fergus about it. Amy wouldn't be happy until she achieved that aim.

True, Steve was satisfied for the time being, but what about when he came of the right age to go to horticultural college? Carly didn't believe in the goodness of the headmaster, or that it would be remembered by the time

Steve reached the right age, and that only left Max's bounty, and how much deeper could they get into his debt?

For the moment, she had forgotten those small envelopes that might be cheques for her uncle's work. They would only be small, anyway, and she hadn't wanted to raise his hopes, but she should have talked to him about them. Forcing herself to be honest, she realised that she had believed them to be somehow part of Max's doing, his influence, and she shrank from the thought. There was the question of little Holly and her singing lessons, too.

She got up slowly. It was no use pushing the thought away from her any longer. She must get herself married. That way, Max would have to take himself out of their lives, and even though she shrank from the thought of Don Foxwell as a husband, Keith Anscombe might not be so bad.

His shop was a reflection of himself, which wasn't surprising, for it was the only thing he had to interest him and he poured himself into it. Carly wondered what had made him get interested in her from the first. His 'courtship', if it could be called that, took the curious form of holding her hand too long when greeting her and saying goodbye, and buying out of hand everything of their handiwork that she offered him, without even considering whether it was what he needed for the shop or not. He had never taken her to dinner or to a show, and now, looking in the window where she could see him reaching to put something back that he had shown a customer, she wondered a little about him. At this moment, with the sunlight slanting right on him for once, she saw that he was not so middle-aged as she had first thought him. He was in his late thirties, but his hair wasn't grey, merely a faded, fair, thinning head of hair that would succumb to premature baldness. His eyes, pale and moist behind his glasses, were of a curious light grey and she had never ever seen them light with any warmth or humour. An earnest man, who took his time to think, took his time to do anything, really. The thing that had always worried her about him, in connection with possible marriage, was how bothered he would be by the children, who were inclined to be vociferous at times and rather boisterous. Impatient, too, with someone like Keith, who took his time in thinking a thought and voicing it.

Keith looked up at that moment, caught sight of her, seemed to be trying to think who she was, then remembering and coming slowly to the door. "Carlotta!" he said, and it struck her that there wasn't much pleasure in his manner, at seeing her.

"Is it an inconvenient time, Keith?" she asked anxiously.

"Not . . . exactly," he said, and looked out into the street. "Are you alone, Carlotta?"

"Yes, of course I am," she laughed. "I've just come from seeing my uncle. At the hospital," she gently reminded him. He certainly seemed distracted.

"Oh, yes, just so," he murmured, then almost pulled her through the shop to the small room at the back. "Sit there while I arrange for the girl to come down and mind the shop while we talk."

'The girl' was a stolid, plain, mousy forty-five but reputed by local gossip to be a good ten years older. Like Keith, she was slow in her movements and thinking, didn't talk much and adequately served him in both office and shop. Carlotta heard him precisely repeating what he wanted her to do and finally he came back to the small sitting-room.

"I'm not myself today," he confessed, with rather more brevity and vigour than usual. "Few people realise I am not strong. I was very upset when the girl told me he'd been in. Fortunately I had just gone out to lunch." He looked sharply at her. "Are you sure you're alone, Carlotta?"

"Yes, of course, Keith! And who is this who came in your absence?"

"Why, Foxwell, the builder, of course. Who else?"

Carlotta could have thought of other people who might have upset Keith, such as the local tax inspector, though why Keith should be upset over his appearance — since he paid his taxes as he should — she couldn't think. "Was he . . . abusive?" she asked carefully. Don Foxwell could be rather unpleasant if he were in a temper. "And what did he want, in this shop? I mean, I wouldn't have thought he'd be interested in . . . "

"Exactly!" Keith took her up, and started what turned out to be the beginning of a series of little forays to the net-curtained window in the door, to peer into the shop. Each customer appeared to alarm him.

"So what did he want?" she persevered.

"You! He seemed to think you'd be here!"

"Well, I don't see why that should upset anyone, even if he did think I'd be here. I mean, he knows I bring our hand-made items to you, to sell for us."

"Yes, and that's another thing. He said when he . . . when you're his wife . . . there would be no more of that trade or he'd . . . my dear, he became quite violent. If the local constable hadn't been passing and heard the girl call out, I can't think what would have happened."

"Did he hit her?" Carlotta was torn between wanting to laugh at the thought of the big Don Foxwell charging into this cluttered shop and scaring Keith's female helper, and feeling uneasy at the possibility that Don might well be of a violent nature in the normal way when things displeased him.

"No. She was just afraid because he was in a threatening mood. He was — ah! — indicating he had heard gossip about you. And me. That we were — ah! — thinking of becoming — man and wife." He avoided Carlotta's eyes and she wondered if people hadn't been a little too quick to jump to this conclusion. She wondered now why Keith Anscombe had ever entered people's minds as a husband for herself, when you considered the noisy lovable household that might be presumed to go with her.

"I'm sorry your clerk was worried by him. I don't think he's really violent. Just not . . . restrained, I suppose." And that didn't sound right.

Keith said, "I'm a peacable man, Carlotta. It's true I've . . . often thought, when you came in here . . . with the hand-made things, and we have talked . . . I mean, the thought of you, sitting by the fire sewing such things, and everyone says you're a wonderful cook, and you seem such a comforting sort of person . . . "

Her mind leapt forward as always and she thought that he was really being very articulate, whatever she had thought in the past. That was how he had actually seen her: a good cook, a comforting woman, one who would use her spare time to continue making hand-made things for his shop. What else would such a man as Keith look for in a wife?

"But I'm not a man of violence, Carlotta, and to be really honest, I don't know how I would figure in a violent scene with such a man as Foxwell. What has given him the idea that he had — ah! — prior claim?"

"I don't know, Keith. I confess it worried me when he was at the house, the day we heard that The Mill House was to be pulled down. I believe that was what upset him. All the work he had put into repairing and adding to it. We only paid him in kind. We hadn't much money and he never sent bills. I didn't think he was scheming on those lines . . . "

"He hasn't already asked you . . . "

"Oh, no," she said firmly, "but . . . the doctor has."

She looked quickly at him. His face registered distinct relief. As she had anticipated, he didn't mind the thought of Guy Morrison as a rival for her affections. Everyone knew the doctor and liked him. Besides, he wouldn't be likely to wreck Keith's shop if he were disappointed. Keith ventured, "And what did you say to him, if I may ask?"

Carlotta's mind was suddenly filled with Max and whether Keith had heard the gossip about him. She said, almost without considering the words, "I refused him. I told him I was keen on someone else."

Keith looked so pleased, she realised with horror what she had done. He would think that she had refused the doctor because of her feelings for Keith. She wasn't a vain girl. Jay was the beauty of the family and they all expected her to be married first, but Carlotta was uncomfortably aware that one could have a certain allure for men who knew one well enough, if one was seen to be a comfortable housekeeper and acknowledged good cook. She felt a little sick. Must she do this? Keith was going to ask her to marry him, she could see that. Could she do this, for her family, for Uncle Fergus, and because Max wasn't free? If only she could have been sure she would never see Max again. No, better still, if only she could go to another district, where nowhere, nothing, would remind her of Max. How could she marry Keith, kind inoffensive Keith, who would probably make her a good if dull husband, and do his duty by the young ones, while the sight of the little stone bridge, the hills, The Mill House itself, even the old bike, would remind her so much of Max, that the knife would turn in her heart a thousand times a day.

She looked up to add quickly that she had decided not to marry anyone when she saw a look of stark horror on Keith's face. He wrenched open the door into the shop, where 'the girl' was serving a woman with a child by her side. The thought flashed through Carly's mind: he's seen Don Foxwell and he's going to clear the shop of customers. She felt a new respect for

Keith, for moving so quickly and for obviously intending to stand up to the burly builder. But things moved so rapidly, then, that she forgot such a thought.

The shop was on the corner. Often she had thought, standing in the window searching for some little thing to buy for someone's gift, that it felt that the traffic coming down the hill to the crossroads on which the shop stood was coming straight into the plate-glass window, but somehow they always seemed to lessen speed enough to make a neat turn and avoid even scratching the shop.

Today it was different. It was Don Foxwell's blue-and-red striped van that Keith had seen, coming at speed down the hill. Whatever Keith had thought or feared, Carly never knew. In the cab of the van, Don Foxwell had been working himself up into a temper because he had felt a fool, not discovering Carly in the studio, and no sign of her having been there lately. He didn't know he'd accidentally set fire to the place, but he

281

did know that Lady Powley must have had no intention of offering him work at Powley Court. She had 'set him up' and probably knew well enough that nobody was in the studio, and had urged him indirectly to force a way in, moreover. He would never get work at Powley Court, he now saw, and there was only one person he wanted to take it out on — Carly. And there was, to his way of thinking, only one place where she would be, since it was too late for her to be at the hospital with her uncle: Keith's shop.

So incensed was he that he forgot the crucial moment most drivers slowed down on that hill, to take the corner. It was as if he had deliberately increased speed, the rate he came at the shop window.

Carly tore through the shop, Keith behind her. She heard things around them being knocked over, as Keith abandoned his usual careful threading way between the small cluttered tables, but it was Carly who got there first, to rip the child from where its mother had sat it — while she examined a breakable object Keith's assistant was showing her, further back in the shop — in an antique oak high chair in the window. But her foot got tangled with some of the plaited ropes of plant-pots Keith had left temporarily on the floor near the door. All she could do was to throw the child towards Keith, before the light was blotted out by Don's van . . .

Carlotta had never been in hospital before and, in the brief moments when she seemed to swim upwards from the merciful oblivion of the drugs she associated with the prick of the needle, she knew she was very badly injured. It was always dark, until one day, feeling less pain than usual, her hand slowly explored and found bandages over her head. I can't see, she thought, her heart hammering madly, and I won't ever walk again. A conviction arising from the dormant fear that had always come out to worry her when she had got overtired. I mustn't ever get ill, she had told herself, because they all need me at The Mill House.

But as always, before she had even a chance to try and ask someone, there was the prick of the needle again and the world of hospital slipped away. But somehow, through the maddeningly slow methods of feeding information to the patient, the truth pierced Carlotta that she had had to have a series of operations, that now it was no longer late summer but the onset of winter and that her uncle was out of convalescence. But here she met a block: nobody mentioned The Mill House. Nobody mentioned Max or the things that had figured so largely in her mind before she had come to this place, such as Keith and his shop, her uncle's writing success or how the children were progressing, for the school term must have started again.

Carly without things to do was a difficult enough person. Carlotta without information or sight of her family and friends was an even more difficult person. Her condition began to deteriorate.

She slept fitfully. One day she awoke to hear someone say, "We shall have to rethink this. We must tell her some things or she'll slip right back."

"Yes, but *what* things?" This was the voice of the ward sister. "If you start answering questions, where will it end?"

"Play it by ear," was the advice of the surgeon whose face had swum constantly into her consciousness.

"And what about Maxstead Jefferson?" This, ah, this was the question Carly wanted answering most, but the two people talking moved away, down the corridor, and all Carly heard was a slightly muffled rise and fall of voices, intermingling with an unfortunate junior dropping a pile of metal B. P.'s in the sluice with a clatter.

Carly buttonholed the Staff Nurse. "I'm not going to be able to walk again, am I?" she demanded.

"Goodness, of course you are!" the nurse smiled. "Is *that* what's worrying you? As a matter of fact, you're going on a ride down the corridor this very day."

"What's been wrong with me, to keep me under for so long?" Carly demanded, but the nurse talked hard as well and she got no answer. But when she was wheeled back to her bed, the nurse said, "Would you feel like a visitor or two? Your uncle, for instance?"

She couldn't believe it, nor could she believe the sight of Fergus, walking into her private room, looking just like he used to. A little more lined and old perhaps, but that was understandable. He had been very ill, of course. She said so.

"So have you, my dear," he said, as he kissed her left cheek. "How are you feeling now?"

"Not so good as I was," she admitted. "They won't tell me anything."

"Well, they don't, do they?" he

286

commiserated. "I know they kept me in the dark until I threatened to get violent.

"In the dark about what?" she asked quickly.

"About everything," he said, after a pause. "It's not that there are secrets, so much as a sort of blanket over news, and then one worries. If only they'd just keep you posted as to what was going on at home — "

And so, with that calm way of dealing with it, he got by on that first visit. "You don't have to worry about not walking again, love, but I warn you, it'll be a long time before you can. The physiotherapists get at you, because it stands to reason, after being so long in bed, you have to have a bit of help."

"Okay, that's fine, now you've explained it. I thought I'd have to be pushed about in a wheelchair for the rest of my days."

He sighed deeply with relief that she had taken his explanation so well. "Anything else you want to know, apart from a report on the activities of the rest of the family, which I will now give you," he said with a broad smile, and so the first visit went off well.

But by the time he came again, she had had time to think. "You didn't mention the accident, and I've got out of them why they cut my hair off and why my head was all bandaged for so long," she said reproachfully.

"Do you remember the accident?" he asked carefully.

"Well, yes, a bit. I'd like to know about the other people, though. Keith was near me. Is he . . . all right?"

"Keith will have to walk with a stick," he said with reluctance. "That heavy chest near the door of the shop fell on him, pinning his leg down. They did a good job on him, though."

"Poor Keith, I think he thought more of that shop than anything."

"He'll be all right financially," Fergus said. "Compensation."

"Funny thing," Carlotta mused, "he ran to save that child without thinking of himself, yet he'd just been telling me that Don Foxwell was likely to threaten him, because of me. I think he was scared of Don. He'd been in the shop and frightened Keith's assistant, while Keith was at lunch." She hesitated. "How did Don come out of it? I don't suppose much was left of his van! "

"He didn't come out of it," Fergus said quietly, knowing Carly would rather have the truth. "It seems, according to young Amy, that Don had been to try and find you, the day you saw me at the hospital. They were on the other side of the stone bridge, and Amy was going back to the house for something, and saw him going away from the studio."

"The studio! But what did he want there, Uncle?"

"Nobody seems to know, but Amy said she saw him come out of the door — was that possible? Hadn't you locked the place that day?"

"Oh, yes, I'd locked it all right," Carly said, but somehow at this distance the studio didn't matter much. What she wanted to know was if Max knew about her accident. She didn't expect to see him, but why didn't he send her flowers, or write? She dared not ask, so she tried something else. "You haven't mentioned Jay. Has Edward asked her to marry him?"

"Yes, but she wanted to wait until you were better, and able to be her matron of honour," he told her.

He wished they'd either tell her everything themselves, or give him permission to. "Your hair looks rather nice, so short," he smiled.

Then he wished he hadn't said that. "Let me see it," she demanded. "There's a small mirror in my handbag."

He drew a deep breath. "Your handbag was damaged. It was on your shoulder, love. It got too ripped to use again. Everything inside was ripped, too. That's what happens in those cases. I'll buy you a new bag for Christmas, if you like. I'm doing well with writing. Got my own space in the local paper now."

Again he had side-tracked her and he went soon afterwards.

Carly lay sweating. Something was wrong. Everyone was trying so hard to pretend nothing was wrong.

The next morning, the orderly on duty was happily swooshing a wet mop over her floor, the cigarette dangling at her lips. "Doing a treat, aren't you, love? Soon be up and out of here, shouldn't wonder."

"I don't think so. But I hope so, or I'll be too late to get a back number of the local newspaper, which will have reported my accident. Keith Anscombe's shop on the corner, you know."

"Oh, *that* was your accident, was it? Well, I never! I've got a copy of that at home. Always keep newspapers with local bits in. I'll bring it up for you, if you like, duck."

So in spite of the scheming of the medical and nursing staff, Carly found herself staring at the wreck that had been poor Keith's own little domain.

The shop on the corner. Carly's stomach turned over as she recalled how near she must have been to that wrecked window and how lucky she was. And then she idly turned the pages of the local paper and found the news of the fire which had burnt out The Mill House, and the strange lonely death of Lady Powley. *So Max was free!*

"But where are you all living?" That was the essential question for Carlotta, when she next saw her uncle and had finished telling him bitterly how she had suffered from being kept in the dark about everything.

"I know, love, but you couldn't be told. You were too ill to take all the shocks. We're all living at Powley Court. Oh, not on the grand scale, so don't get excited. It belongs to Maxstead Jefferson now, and he had one wing altered for us, so it's like our own house. The children love it, because of the animals, and of course Jay's enchanted with the grand piano he bought for her."

"He's still there? At Powley Court? And he hasn't even been to see me?" she whispered.

"Well, he wouldn't come, love, would he? They wouldn't even let poor Keith come in to see you, and he had priority, surely."

Carlotta whitened. "I don't think I understand, Uncle. I *have* seen the notice of Max's wife's death, you know," and she touched the newspaper. "I did rather think that . . . that was the only obstacle."

Fergus looked surprised. "Well, I did, too, at one time, but after what happened the day of the accident . . . "

"What did happen? What do you mean?" she asked blankly.

"You don't remember? Max said he quite understood, but it hasn't stopped him from pushing the sales of your Jack-and-Mack series, and he's hoping you'll do some more pictures for it as soon as you can, and he's also arranging to have The Mill House rebuilt, because he seems to think you'd like it."

"But I don't understand. *What* happened on the day of the accident to make Max change? At least, I *thought* he cared for me."

"Well, Keith of course. He said you turned someone else down because you wanted *him*." Fergus looked sharply at her. "Isn't that true, love?"

"Yes, it's true, but I didn't mean . . . Oh, he must have misunderstood," she fretted. "I seem to remember telling him of course I didn't want Don Foxwell, but the doctor had proposed to me and I'd turned him down because I cared for someone else."

"And Keith thought you meant him? Well, I suppose he would," Fergus said slowly. "You've known him so long, and you're always so nice to him when you meet."

"I was sorry for him. He seemed so defenceless, and he was rather scared at the thought of Don Foxwell threatening him that day. But I never gave him cause to think I . . . " She bit her lip, remembering that day when it seemed that as Max was married, she must make a push to marry someone else, for all sorts of reasons but mainly to convince Max that he must go out of their lives. And now Keith expected her to stand by what she had suggested!

"Oh, well, I don't suppose it will matter," she said. "But I wish we didn't have to thank Max for so much of his generosity. After all, it's his wife's money he's using . . . "

"Carly, my dear, when will you understand that it's no such thing?" Fergus protested. "He was a very rich man when he first made our acquaintance, and he had made himself rich by his own ideas and sticking at it. A self-made man, if ever there was one, and you did nothing but deride him every time he tried to tell you!"

"I didn't believe it. I thought he was boasting, talking big," she said miserably. "And now I've lost him."

"Well, Keith is hammering to see you. What will you do about that?"

"Oh, I'll see him, I suppose," Carlotta

said. "Poor Keith, yes, I'll see him."

Fergus still hesitated. He had suddenly noticed two shadows moving on the other side of the frosted-glass partition and realised that Carly's two male visitors had been allowed up to wait outside: Keith because he had said he was engaged to Carly, and Max because . . . well, they wouldn't refuse him, would they, after what he was doing for this wing of the hospital. Fergus felt that he couldn't go out of this room without making a push of some sort to take away the stark misery in Carlotta's face.

"My dear, before I go, tell me, just tell me in confidence, which of those two you really care for and would want to spend the rest of your life with? Marriage should be for ever, you know."

"I must marry Keith, if I said so. I can't go back on that!" she gasped, reproachfully.

"But if you had your choice," he insisted.

"Oh, Uncle, you know it's Max. It has been since I first saw him and had a fight with him. It has been all along. It always will be. You must know that," and her voice broke.

"Then will you be being fair to poor Keith, if that's the way you feel in your heart?" he said gently.

But he didn't have to say any more, for after the slightest hesitation, one of the shadows melted away. Unfortunately, at that moment, the hospital sounds had abated and Carly heard the limping footsteps, as he went away. "Uncle, was that Keith? Oh, you did it on purpose! How could you?"

"I did it for you, my dear. No, for Max, too. The two nearest my heart," he murmured, almost too low for her to hear, as he went quickly to the door and opened it.

Max strode in. He was still a big man but he had lost weight and he didn't look well. She struggled up on her elbows at the sight of him. She wasn't looking her best. She didn't know it, but short hair didn't suit her, in spite of what her uncle had said. And she, too, had lost a lot of weight. But, Fergus thought, as he glanced at both of their faces before leaving them, they both still looked as if they were aglow with their love for each other: two people about to be fused into one. He went quietly out.

There was no sound of voices. They said nothing, though he waited for a moment to be sure it was all right.

Sister rustled past him and opened the door. Over her shoulder he got a glance of them, locked in a tight embrace. No words had been said. They had just 'homed' to each other and were holding each other tightly, as though fearing that they would any moment be torn apart.

Sister frowned and pulled the door to and turned to him. "I shall give them ten minutes," she said severely. "Meantime you, Mr Buckland, if your conscience can stand it, will come and take tea with me in my office, and have a little talk, for I should like very much to know how you have achieved that miracle."

THE END

WITH SOMEBODY ELSE
Theresa Charles

Rosamond sets off for Cornwall with Hugo to meet his family, blissfully unaware of the shocks in store for her.

A SUMMER FOR STRANGERS
Claire Hamilton

Because she had lost her job, her flat and she had no money, Tabitha agreed to pose as Adam's future wife although she believed the scheme to be deceitful and cruel.

VILLA OF SINGING WATER
Angela Petron

The disquieting incidents that occurred at the Vatican and the Colosseum did not trouble Jan at first, but then they became increasingly unpleasant and alarming.

DOCTOR NAPIER'S NURSE
Pauline Ash

When cousins Midge and Derry are entered as probationer nurses on the same day but at different hospitals they agree to exchange identities.

A GIRL LIKE JULIE
Louise Ellis

Caroline absolutely adored Hugh Barrington, but then Julie Crane came into their lives. Julie was the kind of girl who attracts men without even trying.

COUNTRY DOCTOR
Paula Lindsay

When Evan Richmond bought a practice in a remote country village he did not realise that a casual encounter would lead to the loss of his heart.

ENCORE
Helga Moray

Craig and Janet realise that their true happiness lies with each other, but it is only under traumatic circumstances that they can be reunited.

NICOLETTE
Ivy Preston

When Grant Alston came back into her life, Nicolette was faced with a dilemma. Should she follow the path of duty or the path of love?

THE GOLDEN PUMA
Margaret Way

Catherine's time was spent looking after her father's Queensland farm. But what life was there without David, who wasn't interested in her?

HOSPITAL BY THE LAKE
Anne Durham

Nurse Marguerite Ingleby was always ready to become personally involved with her patients, to the despair of Brian Field, the Senior Surgical Registrar, who loved her.

VALLEY OF CONFLICT
David Farrell

Isolated in a hostel in the French Alps, Ann Russell sees her fiancé being seduced by a young girl. Then comes the avalanche that imperils their lives.

NURSE'S CHOICE
Peggy Gaddis

A proposal of marriage from the incredibly handsome and wealthy Reagan was enough to upset any girl — and Brooke Martin was no exception.

A DANGEROUS MAN
Anne Goring

Photographer Polly Burton was on safari in Mombasa when she met enigmatic Leon Hammond. But unpredictability was the name of the game where Leon was concerned.

PRECIOUS INHERITANCE
Joan Moules

Karen's new life working for an authoress took her from Sussex to a foreign airstrip and a kidnapping; to a real life adventure as gripping as any in the books she typed.

VISION OF LOVE
Grace Richmond

When Kathy takes over the rundown country kennels she finds Alec Stinton, a local vet, very helpful. But their friendship arouses bitter jealousy and a tragedy seems inevitable.

CRUSADING NURSE
Jane Converse

It was handsome Dr. Corbett who opened Nurse Susan Leighton's eyes and who set her off on a lonely crusade against some powerful enemies and a shattering struggle against the man she loved.

WILD ENCHANTMENT
Christina Green

Rowan's agreeable new boss had a dream of creating a famous perfume using her precious Silverstar, but Rowan's plans were very different.

DESERT ROMANCE
Irene Ord

Sally agrees to take her sister Pam's place as La Chartreuse the dancer, but she finds out there is more to it than dyeing her hair red and looking like her sister.

HEART OF ICE
Marie Sidney

How was January to know that not only would the warmth of the Swiss people thaw out her frozen heart, but that she too would play her part in helping someone to live again?

LUCKY IN LOVE
Margaret Wood

Companion-secretary to wealthy gambler Laura Duxford, who lived in Monaco, seemed to Melanie a fabulous job. Especially as Melanie had already lost her heart to Laura's son, Julian.

NURSE TO PRINCESS JASMINE
Lilian Woodward

Nick's surgeon brother, Tom, performs an operation on an Arabian princess, and she invites Tom, Nick and his fiancé to Omander, where a web of deceit and intrigue closes about them.

THE WAYWARD HEART
Eileen Barry

Disaster-prone Katherine's nickname was "Kate Calamity", but her boss went too far with an outrageous proposal, which because of her latest disaster, she could not refuse.

FOUR WEEKS IN WINTER
Jane Donnelly

Tessa wasn't looking forward to meeting Paul Mellor again — she had made a fool of herself over him once before. But was Orme Jared's solution to her problem likely to be the right one?

SURGERY BY THE SEA
Sheila Douglas

Medical student Meg hadn't really wanted to go and work with a G.P. on the Welsh coast although the job had its compensations. But Owen Roberts was certainly not one of them!

HEAVEN IS HIGH
Anne Hampson

The new heir to the Manor of Marbeck had been found. But it was rather unfortunate that when he arrived unexpectedly he found an uninvited guest, complete with stetson and high boots.

LOVE WILL COME
Sarah Devon

June Baker's boss was not really her idea of her ideal man, but when she went from third typist to boss's secretary overnight she began to change her mind.

ESCAPE TO ROMANCE
Kay Winchester

Oliver and Jean first met on Swale Island. They were both trying to begin their lives afresh, but neither had bargained for complications from the past.

CASTLE IN THE SUN
Cora Mayne

Emma's invalid sister, Kym, needed a warm climate, and Emma jumped at the chance of a job on a Mediterranean island. But Emma soon finds that intrigues and hazards lurk on the sunlit isle.

BEWARE OF LOVE
Kay Winchester

Carol Brampton resumes her nursing career when her family is killed in a car accident. With Dr. Patrick Farrell she begins to pick up the pieces of her life, but is bitterly hurt when insinuations are made about her to Patrick.

DARLING REBEL
Sarah Devon

When Jason Farradale's secretary met with an accident, her glamorous stand-in was quite unable to deal with one problem in particular.

THE PRICE OF PARADISE
Jane Arbor

It was a shock to Fern to meet her estranged husband on an island in the middle of the Indian Ocean, but to discover that her father had engineered it puzzled Fern. What did he hope to achieve?

DOCTOR IN PLASTER
Lisa Cooper

When Dr. Scott Sutcliffe is injured, Nurse Caroline Hurst has to cope with a very demanding private case. But when she realises her exasperating patient has stolen her heart, how can Caroline possibly stay?

A TOUCH OF HONEY
Lucy Gillen

Before she took the job as secretary to author Robert Dean, Cadie had heard how charming he was, but that wasn't her first impression at all.

ROMANTIC LEGACY
Cora Mayne

As kennelmaid to the Armstrongs, Ann Brown, had no idea that she would become the central figure in a web of mystery and intrigue.

THE RELENTLESS TIDE
Jill Murray

Steve Palmer shared Nurse Marie Blane's love of the sea and small boats. Marie's other passion was her step-brother. But when danger threatened who should she turn to — her step-brother or the man who stirred emotions in her heart?

ROMANCE IN NORWAY
Cora Mayne

Nancy Crawford hopes that her visit to Norway will help her to start life again. She certainly finds many surprises there, including unexpected happiness.

UNLOCK MY HEART
Honor Vincent

When Ruth Linton, a young widow with three children, inherits a house in the country, it seems to be the answer to her dreams. But Ruth's problems were only just beginning . . .

SWEET PROMISE
Janet Dailey

Erica had met Rafael in Mexico, where their relationship had been brief but dramatic. Now, over a year later in Texas, she had met him again — and he had the power to wreck her life.

SAFARI ENCOUNTER
Rosemary Carter

Jenny had to accept that she couldn't run her father's game park alone; so she let forceful Joshua Adams virtually take over. But Joshua took over her heart as well!

SHADOW DANCE
Margaret Way

When Carl Danning sent her to interview Richard Kauffman, Alix was far from pleased — but the assignment led her to help Richard repair the situation between him and his ex-wife.

WHITE HIBISCUS
Rosemary Pollock

"A boring English model with dubious morals," was how Count Paul Santana Demajo described Emma. But what about the Count's morals, and who is Marianne?

STARS THROUGH THE MIST
Betty Neels

Secretly in love with Gerard van Doordninck, Deborah should have been thrilled when he asked her to marry him. But he only wanted a wife for practical not romantic reasons.